The Best Possible Experience

"A full-hearted, brilliant debut full of necessary beauty. Injam writes of longing, of love, of home, and of the Indian diaspora, and as one reads the stories, they find that together they create an epic mosaic of life."   —Nana Kwame Adjei-Brenyah, author of *Chain-Gang All-Stars*

"In Injam's enthralling, deeply intimate stories, characters contend with what it takes to survive grief, heartbreak, disappointment, another culture, and each other. . . . An exquisite debut!"   —Deesha Philyaw, author of *The Secret Lives of Church Ladies*

"In these wise, intricate stories, Nishanth Injam shows us, with lancing clarity, the shame and embarrassment of immigration, the ways in which relationships form and dissolve around silences. . . . An arresting new voice in contemporary Indian—and American—fiction."   —Karan Mahajan, author of *The Association of Small Bombs*

"A gorgeous and devastating portrait of what it costs, literally and psychically, to make a new life away from home. Injam has a gift for capturing complex characters facing the unsettling strangeness of unfamiliar places and increasingly unfamiliar selves. . . . A graceful and sophisticated debut from a wonderful new writer."   —Danielle Evans, author of *The Office of Historical Corrections*

"These hauntingly beautiful stories of arrivals and departures, of love and loss, are a reminder of the transporting power of fiction. *The Best Possible Experience* is quite possibly the best debut collection of the year."   —Peter Ho Davies, author of
A Lie Someone Told You About Yourself

"Alive with vivid, vibrant, and affecting writing. . . . This collection is truly a can't-miss release."   —*Chicago Review of Books*

"Perceptive and penetrating. . . . A quietly powerful look at a fundamental human desire—for a sense of home, a place to belong. . . . Masterful descriptions convey their heart-rending memories and hard-hitting emotions. An enlightening collection. . . . A must for readers who loved Mohsin Hamid's *The Reluctant Fundamentalist* and Samanta Schweblin's *Seven Empty Houses.*"   —*BookPage* (starred review)

"Eleven gems make up Injam's stellar debut short-story collection showcasing exquisite quotidian beauty haunted by seemingly inevitable loss."   —*Booklist* (starred review)

"Dynamic and insightful. . . . This is a triumph."
          —*Publishers Weekly* (starred review)

Nishanth Injam

The Best Possible Experience

Nishanth Injam received an MFA from the Helen Zell Writers' Program at the University of Michigan. He received a PEN/ Robert J. Dau Short Story Prize for Emerging Writers and a Cecelia Joyce Johnson Award from the Key West Literary Seminar. His work has appeared in *The Virginia Quarterly Review*, *Zoetrope*, *The Georgia Review* (which won the 2022 ASME Award for Fiction for its publication of his story), *Best Debut Short Stories 2021*, and *The Best American Magazine Writing 2022*. Raised in Telangana, India, he now lives in Illinois.

The Best Possible Experience

Stories

Nishanth Injam

Vintage Books
A Division of Penguin Random House LLC
New York

FIRST VINTAGE BOOKS EDITION 2024

"The Math of Living" originally appeared in *VQR* (Winter 2020)
and in *Best Debut Short Stories 2021* (Catapult, 2021). "Come with Me"
originally appeared in *The Georgia Review* (Summer 2021) and in *Best
American Magazine Writing 2022* (Columbia University Press, 2022).

The Library of Congress has cataloged the Pantheon edition as follows:
Name: Injam, Nishanth, author.
Title: The best possible experience : stories / Nishanth Injam.
Other titles: Best possible experience (Compilation)
Description: First edition. | New York : Pantheon Books, 2023
Identifiers: LCCN 2022042230 (print). LCCN 2022042231 (ebook).
Subjects: LCGFT: Short stories.
Classification: LCC PS3609.N53 B47 2023 (print) | LCC PS3609.N53
(ebook) DDC 813/.6—dc23
LC record available at https://lccn.loc.gov/2022042230
LC ebook record available at https://lccn.loc.gov/2022042231

Vintage Books Trade Paperback ISBN: 978-0-593-47023-7
eBook ISBN: 978-0-593-31770-9

vintagebooks.com

Printed in the United States of America
10 9 8 7 6 5 4 3 2 1

For my parents—
one across oceans and
the other below earth,
always lighthouses

What he sought was always something lying ahead, and even if it was a matter of the past it was a past that changed gradually as he advanced on his journey.

—Italo Calvino, *Invisible Cities*

CONTENTS

The Best Possible Experience

The Bus

The bus has a bathroom. Other buses that leave Bengaluru for my hometown don't have bathrooms. They pull over on the highway when you have to pee, or they stop at a dhaba and the driver asks passengers to go so he won't have to make extra stops along the way.

The bus is a luxury coach, dark brown from the outside. It has a thirty-two-inch TV and reclining seats and air-conditioning, all of which makes me think: *What a good deal.* It's the Diwali weekend and every long-distance coach is full of techies going home. Securing a ticket was impossible, but then I came across a new office at the back of the bus station, a travel company by the name of Alphonso Tours, and they made it happen.

The driver is busy tinkering with a hearing aid as I get on the bus. "Don't use the bathroom for number two. Only number one," he says, not bothering to look up.

I feel the air-conditioning already—sweet. The bus is nearly full. I look at my ticket: 20B. An aisle seat next to a bearded man on his phone, music blasting out of his earbuds. I sit down and relax my feet and begin watching the Bollywood film playing on the TV, a film in which the hero shoves the heroine from the roof of a tall building. Nothing like a movie to alleviate the boredom of an overnight bus ride. We're past the outskirts of the city now, and farmland has started to appear on either side of the road. I haven't gone home in months, and I'm torn—can you tell, K?

An hour passes. The bearded man takes a selfie and posts it on Instagram. I turn my neck to stretch, and the seat behind me is empty. I remember seeing an old woman with a large nose there, and I can't tell if she's moved to a different seat or if I'm confusing her with someone I know from somewhere else. My eyes fall on the bathroom; that's it. She's gone to the restroom. But then a passenger in the front, a burly man in 5D, stands up and closes the bathroom door behind him. I turn to my back and count six empty seats in the dark. I don't remember seeing so many empty seats when I got on. Weird. Must be exhaustion. I continue watching the movie.

Five minutes later my eyes drift toward the bathroom. The burly man still hasn't come out. 5D is empty and I'm disgusted. This man hasn't listened to what the driver said. Instead, he's taking an extraordinary dump. People are like that, I guess.

A lot of passengers are sleeping, some snoring. The bearded man next to me is watching a YouTube video on his phone: a man keeps springing a toy snake in people's faces and capturing their reactions. My neighbor laughs whenever the prank results in an especially outsized response.

I try sleeping, but the movie is loud.

I take deep breaths, but sleep doesn't come. I can sleep on the bus only if I'm in a window seat. You know that, K. You must remember the time we went on a school picnic and you took the window seat, not on the way to the orchard but on the way back home. Our bellies were stuffed with mangoes, and I told you the bus would make me puke if I didn't have the window and you called my bluff and we fought over it. God, the kids we were, it wasn't a pretty sight. You were stronger than me and you felt that you'd won, but I clutched at my throat and retched hard enough for some phlegm to fall on my shorts. You were sorry; you gave me the window seat and offered the kerchief Mom tucked in your shirt pocket. When I began to feel the mangoes in my throat, you told me to take deep breaths and sleep until the feeling subsided. I remember your face, blank, staring ahead, thinking who knows what, as I sloped against the window, falling asleep. Now you're dead and I'm stuck on this bus.

It's nothing new. You've been dead for a while, long enough for me to nod when people ask if I'm an only child. Long enough for me to forget that I had a brother. When you're twenty-three, everything that happened in childhood feels like a lifetime ago. That's just the way it is. Sorry, K. I don't think of you often. Except when I'm on a bus and I'm going home, and what home is has changed irrevocably, not because I live and work in Bengaluru now, away from our parents, although I shouldn't say our parents because they're not the parents you'd remember, they're my parents now, and I promise there's no satisfaction in claiming them for myself. It's just that people change and they're not who they were, nobody is, and that's what I'm trying to say, that life has changed for all of us, and home has too. We no longer live in the one-bedroom apartment on the hill; we fell to the ghetto soon after you died. What home is has changed so much that I don't even know how to define it, but here I am, just thinking about all the ways it's changed, and you, K, are on the top of that precipice.

The first thing anyone sees at home is a garlanded photo taken on your tenth birthday. You're grinning stupidly and making a victory sign. It might be the only photo of you that doesn't include me. Did you know that Mom doesn't make beef curry anymore because she can't stop herself from bringing up the fact that you used to gnaw at the shin like a dog? Or that Dad carries a passport photograph of you in his wallet to remind himself that if he'd had enough money, he'd have been able to afford the surgery for your head injury? After you died, I became the center of attention. Not right away, of course, but with time, which is what I'd always wanted, but not like that. You were always their favorite, you could make them laugh, make them feel like parents. I just make them feel like needy children now. I send them money, but I never answer their calls or tell them about my life in the city. What's there to tell? I don't go home except when Mom pleads and pleads. When I'm home, how can I ignore your stupid grin? How can I take their attention all for myself? I never have this problem in the city. There, people just see me as me; they don't think of me as a stand-in for the other.

I open my eyes. 5D is still empty. Has the burly man passed out on the toilet and hurt himself? Then the bathroom door slides open, as though the person who last used it failed to latch it properly. The room is empty. Where has he gone?

I walk to 5D and find a jute bag with some clothes tucked underneath the man's seat. The old man in 5C looks at me questioningly, as if I'm trying to steal 5D's belongings.

"Where is he?" I point at the empty seat.

"What?" 5C says, straining to hear me over the film score.

"The man who was sitting here, where did he go?"

"Toilet," 5C says, his eyes traveling to the half-open bathroom door. He stands up. "Babu?" He looks up and down the aisle. "Where did Babu go?"

"Are you two related?"

"He's my son." 5C steps into the aisle, using his cane. "Babu?"

I feel bad for worrying him. "He's probably just chatting with the driver. I can check."

"The toilet," he says, as if he must pee first.

On the TV, the hero is dancing with the heroine in the Alps. The heroine is not wearing a lot of clothing but the hero has a down coat. I watch them gyrate. The movie is old; I've seen it before. I sit in 5D and wait for the old man to return. I'm used to waiting. It's what I do for work. I spend hours on call providing technical support for Bank of America's internal ticketing system. I sit in meetings all night listening to the front-end team onshore and pick up phrases like "have a good weekend," "knock on wood," "tell me about it."

The song ends and the couple jumps from dancing in the Alps to the confines of an apartment in Mumbai. Remember when we joked about that, K? You said that only ghosts can travel that quickly, and you made creepy whistling noises. I asked you to stop, but you wouldn't. I said I'd tell Mom if you didn't stop, but you kept doing it. I was angry with you; I said I'd cut your tongue off when you were sleeping. There are a lot of things I wish I hadn't said.

Do you remember too the time we played hide-and-seek behind the portico and you crouched down in the well and covered yourself with coconut leaves? We were all so worried, and when we called your name, you wouldn't answer, and it took a long time for you to emerge, and when you did, you were oddly quiet, not really celebrating the fact that you'd won. Mom abandoned the peanuts she was roasting to fret over you, to check for bruises, and you smiled and brushed her away, but now I wonder if you knew something back then, something unexplainable.

And when it was my time to hide, I ran away to the next street, aiming to do one better than you. When I came back twenty minutes later, you and Mom were striking the TV, trying to make it work. Even after I announced I was back, Mom did nothing, she just said, "Good," and went into the kitchen. You casually asked where I'd been, as if you were trying to be nice, but you were more excited to see a flash of *Tom and Jerry* than you were to talk to me. I unplugged the TV and ran to Mom, sure that you'd chase me, and when you did chase, it was me who smiled from behind Mom's saree this time. Maybe I too knew something back then. I don't think I did, but it's too eerie, the way we were smiling. It's almost as if we both knew where we were headed, as if we both had a sense of what was waiting for us, as if we were practicing our futures, you under the ground, and me far away, hiding from what you'd do to me. Is there a better definition of home than that?

My head hurts. The old man hasn't returned yet. I'm about to get up and knock on the bathroom door to ask if he's okay when it slides open. The bathroom looks empty. I approach gingerly, as though it holds a ghost, and I see the toilet and a sink the size of cupped palms. The bathroom is windowless and smaller than my cubicle. I don't have to step inside to know that the old man isn't there.

I go back to seat 5D. I find the old man's Aadhaar card and medication inside his jute bag. His name is Pulliah; he's seventy-six years old, has a mole on his right cheek, is five feet eight inches tall, and lives in Kadapa. That's him in the photo. I pinch myself and wince in pain. Everything is real and two men have gone missing.

I'm about to walk up to the driver when I see a woman in a red saree, 7B, moving toward the bathroom. Oh fuck.

I stop her. "Madam, please don't use this bathroom."

She looks at me like I'm a creep. "It's empty."

"An old man went in there—" I start to say.

"Disgusting."

She walks to her seat, pauses for a minute, and heads back to the bathroom.

"Madam, trust me, please don't go," I say.

"I have to go, move."

The bald man in 5B stands up. He's been watching us. "Is there a problem?"

"He's telling me not to go to the bathroom," the woman says.

"You have a problem with ladies using the bathroom?"

"Sir, it's not like that. It's not safe," I say, turning toward the bald man.

"Oh," the bald man exclaims. "Safe for men, but not safe for women?"

The woman tries to go to the bathroom, but I stick my hand out, blocking her path.

"What are you doing?" the woman says.

"I'll call the police," the bald man says.

"No, sir, listen to me."

He slaps my arm down and says to the woman, "Madam, you can go. I'll deal with this rascal."

"Please don't go," I say when 5B shoves me, and I fall into the empty seat of 5D. The woman locks the bathroom door behind her.

A different movie has begun playing on the TV. In this one, the hero comes from an affectionate family. Everyone loves him, which can only mean something will go wrong. But the few people who are awake are watching me and 5B instead of the movie. "Sir, please listen to me," I say.

"Sure, you tell me. Which police station do you want to go to?" He takes out his phone.

"The old man who was sitting in this seat here went to the bathroom and didn't come out again."

"What?" he says.

"Yes, sir, I saw him go inside, but he never came out."

"How can he hide in the bathroom?"

5B's eyes light up. He turns to the guy next to him in 5A and says, "Mental."

They soften, urge me to go back to my seat.

I grab 5C's Aadhaar card and say, "This old man is missing. He was sitting there."

They look at me like I'm in the business of stealing Aadhaar cards. "Go to your seat. If you so much as move, we'll call the police."

I don't know what to say; I trudge back to my seat. As soon as I sit, the bearded man wakes up. He looks at the TV and shakes his head: "This movie is terrible."

I agree and introduce myself. His name is Deepak, and he works at Accenture; the bus won't reach his town until four in the morning. We talk a little about our projects, about how crazy our clients are. Deepak says one client made him move a button from one corner of the screen to another three times. "And we had a meeting each time to review the button change!"

I tell him how a white colleague keeps asking me, whenever there's a meeting and no one knows what to say in the beginning, if I know a certain Alex who worked out of Bengaluru. When I tell him that I don't, he says, "Yes, of course not, over a *billion* people there!"

Deepak laughs and opens WhatsApp. I look away.

5B is hovering by the bathroom. The bathroom door has slid open and there's no trace of the woman. I feel relieved but also guilty. Before I have a chance to say anything, 5B walks inside the bathroom and begins examining the hinges. The door bolts shut.

I'm not surprised when it slides open a minute later and 5B is gone. Next to me, Deepak takes a phone call. He says he'll reach home at four in the morning. I'm tempted to say, *How can you be so sure, brother?*

The bus moves on the highway as though it's floating— there's hardly a lurch. The TV's off now; people are sleeping. Deepak is hugging himself, yawning. "It's very cold," he says. The air-conditioning has been working well, maybe too well. I'm beginning to feel my bladder, like I could pee. My town, the first stop, is still three hours away. Can I hold it till then? What the fuck is wrong with this bus, K? Is that why there are so many empty seats?

I watch 18A, a man my age, heading to the bathroom. I don't want to sit back and watch people march toward their death; I want to do something. Deepak is on Facebook, looking at funny videos, when I try to recruit him. "Do you see that man?" I say, pointing toward 18A.

"Yes, why?"

18A closes the bathroom door behind him, and I catch his face: thin mustache, glasses, and spiked hair. "He won't come back from the bathroom," I say.

Deepak says, "What?"

"I know it sounds crazy, but I promise, it's true."

Deepak says, "Oh, is someone already in there?"

I can't believe that I've actually found someone who under-stands that no one is coming out of that bathroom. "Yes—"

"I knew about planes, but I didn't know these things happen on buses too."

"This happens on planes?"

"Oh yes." Deepak's face lights up and he begins filming on his phone.

"What's that for?"

"Proof," Deepak says.

I nod. "Good call, I didn't think of that."

"Also for fun," Deepak adds.

I don't understand what's fun about people disappearing, but I let it go.

Seconds pass. Deepak turns to me and asks, "Was it a woman? The one who was in the bathroom?"

I remember the woman in 7B. "Yes."

"Cool."

"There were also two men before her," I say.

Deepak seems shocked. "They're all in there together?"

"I don't know. I think so," I say.

"Whoa," he says.

I keep my eyes locked to the bathroom. A minute passes.

"Is this for real?" Deepak says.

The bathroom door slides open. 18A is gone. "There! Did you catch that?" I say.

"What the hell?"

Deepak wants to get out into the aisle, so I step aside. I hover behind him, thinking of showing the video to the driver and getting off the bus.

Deepak walks toward the bathroom.

"Don't," I say.

"If I upload this video, I'll get crazy views," Deepak says. He wants to film the inside of the bathroom and make some cash.

"You'll die before you'll be able to," I say.

Deepak laughs. "There has to be a secret compartment," he says, and starts moving.

I hold him and don't let him go. "It's too dangerous," I say. "You'll die."

Deepak kicks me in the leg and wrenches himself free.

A kid, 8C, makes for the bathroom. We run toward the boy, shouting, "No."

The boy turns around.

"Don't go to the bathroom," I say.

"We have a video," Deepak says.

5A gets up. "Oh, great, two mental people."

I shake my fingers at the boy. "Don't."

The boy holds the bathroom handle and watches us. I run toward the kid, dashing past Deepak, accidentally knocking his phone to the floor. The boy's eyes widen; he's scared of us. He locks himself in the bathroom. Deepak holds up his phone; the screen is broken.

8D, the kid's mother, runs from her seat. People wake up and step into the aisle, stifling their yawns and looking at her with interest.

"What did you do to him?" 8D asks me on her way to the bathroom. "Open the door," she says to her son.

The bathroom door opens, and she barges in.

I collapse on the floor as people surge toward the bathroom.

The first time I encountered death, it was a kid three classes above. Pratham, wasn't that his name, K? He wasn't as tall as you were; he drowned in the river. The news came to us in bits and pieces. We learned that he'd been swimming and that the current had been too swift. For weeks after, we passed by his bench and whispered, *"This is where the boy who died used to sit."* For a while, we listened to our parents and avoided the river. Then we forgot about it.

The second time I encountered death, it was a cranky relative in his nineties. We skipped school to go to his last rites. We sat under a tent and played marbles. We ate goat blood fry for lunch and went back home. Death, we learned, could be joyful. For a while, we wanted more people to die.

The third time I encountered death, it was you. I didn't see you fall headfirst from the tall boulder we climbed. I didn't see you bleed at the hospital. I didn't see much of that day. For a while, I saw only Mom shaking her head in anger when I ran for help: "What did you do now? What did you do to him?"

There are four people left on the bus: me, Deepak, 32A, 23C. Deepak is trying to send the video to 32A so he can watch it on his phone and understand. 23C saw the bathroom pilgrimage, the way people kept rushing in after the kid's mother, the way it took them all. "It's evil Shaitan," he says.

"No. It's a Mohini ghost," Deepak says.

32A has slept through the whole thing; he isn't sure if we're pranking him. "Really?"

"Let's get off the bus," I say. "We'll go to the driver and tell him to stop."

23C looks at the bathroom, clearly worried about the fact that we have to pass by it to get off the bus. Deepak says we can shout.

We yell for the driver to stop, as loud as we can. I yell so hard my ears ring and my throat hurts. The driver doesn't turn his head. I remember his hearing aid.

"He can't hear us," I say. I can see the driver's back, his head, but in the rearview mirror, I don't see his eyes. 23C can't tell if that's because the lighting is too dark or because his eye sockets are empty. Either way, 23C is sweating.

"We've no choice," Deepak says.

As we approach the bathroom, Deepak trips on a bag poking out into the aisle and falls on the floor. His shoulder bangs against the hard edge of a seat and he screams. He extends his hand, wincing in pain, and his fingers nearly touch the bathroom door. We're asking if he's okay when Deepak goes hand-first, is sucked into the bathroom with the force of a vacuum cleaner. The whooshing sound that accompanies this force makes me shiver. Deepak yells, his face scrunching, and we grasp at his legs in vain. The bathroom door shuts, and the yelling gradually dies down. An eerie silence remains.

We run back, the three of us. "It's safer if we stay here," I say, still thinking about Deepak and the phone call he took. Someone who cares about him, waiting at the bus station in his town. Why must people die, K?

32A doesn't need the video anymore; he understands. He begins chanting prayers. He says, "I will burst a thousand coconuts at the Tirupati Balaji if I get out alive."

23C wants to throw something at the driver, catch his attention. I'm okay with that plan, but 32A is too scared to do anything that could potentially make the driver take his eyes off the road. We decide not to risk it and designate the last row as our peeing area. The seats 30A, 30B, and 30C become ours. We don't know the first thing about one another—we're just numbers on a bus. A population of three.

The bus gets colder and colder at the back, and I can sense that it's warmer near the bathroom. I wonder if the bus is determined to lure us toward the front. We open people's bags and take out more clothes to wear. We layer up and huddle together.

I look outside and recognize where we are. I'm not far from home. "We just have to wait it out," I say. Two more hours.

"How do we know that the bus will stop?" 32A asks.

I see a sedan to my right and shout, "Help!"

The sedan overtakes the bus.

"They can't hear," 23C says.

"The glass is too thick," 32A says.

"Let's break the emergency glass and jump," 23C says.

I don't want to be roadkill. We will break our legs at the very least. But I don't know what else we can do—I look for something sharp and find a flashlight instead.

Abruptly, the TV comes on. A new movie begins playing.

I haven't seen this one. There's no title, and the footage is grainy. Two kids are playing on a hill. One of them is slightly taller than the other.

The younger one climbs on a tall boulder and says, "I bet you can't do that."

"Let's go home," the older one says, looking at his watch.

"Haha, I know you can't," the younger one says.

The older one climbs on the boulder. His shoe nearly slips, but he holds on and gets to his brother. There's not a whole lot of standing space on the boulder. "Happy?" he says.

I can't watch anymore; I go after the TV with the flashlight. "Come back," I hear 23C and 32A say. I fling the flashlight at the TV, but nothing happens to the screen. It continues to play. The younger one is laughing as the older one puts a hand on his shoulder and says, "I've waited long enough, let's go."

The younger kid lightly shoves the older one, saying, "You go," and the older kid loses his balance, falling to the ground headfirst.

The younger one opens his mouth to scream: "K—"

I'm going, K. I walk into the bathroom saying, "I'm sorry, I'm sorry." I turn around and see 23C and 32A, their eyes switching between the TV and me, faces growing longer and longer.

They've seen the movie. They know my story, they know who I am.

The bathroom door shuts. Shall we go home, brother?

Come with Me

The first time I saw Salim, it was summer. The weather report called it one of Karimnagar's hottest summers. Streets bore silence like a curfew. Cows belched and jutted out their tongues for moisture. The ice cream vendor rolled his cart into the shade of the big peepal tree and fanned himself with a wet cloth. The vegetable market vanished at noon and reappeared in the evening. None of this bothered us; we were boys with cricket on our minds.

I was no star, but I had a good arm and could sometimes take a running catch. Most of us were thirteen, but there were a few who were older. We were forming teams, deciding who'd get to bat first, and we didn't see him approach, heard him before we saw him.

"I got the bat."

I turned and stood transfixed. Salim wore a graphic T-shirt that said ROCKSTAR. Although it was hot and humid, he had worn a leather biker jacket that he took off and folded. His taut biceps glistened. It was a revelation; I had no idea that sweat could look so good. He was older, eighteen or so. He had thin lips, strong thighs, and a sharp nose. I felt my stomach flip and flip, like dice that wouldn't stop rolling.

Salim shook hands with some of the older boys he seemed to

know, greeting them with a generic "Aur, bhai." We drew close to introduce ourselves, and it was apparent he was the sun and the rest of us mere planets.

When it was my turn, I told him my name. Salim ran his fingers through his hair and said, "Khan, Salim Khan."

"Like James Bond?" I had seen a James Bond movie on the neighbors' television and so was aware of this particular mannerism.

"Whatever," he said in a low-pitched voice. But a quick upward dash of his eyebrows all but told me that I was on his radar now. I couldn't stop smiling.

"Chal, start," the boys screamed, and we were off. Salim was on my team, and I watched him field in the short cover position. Hips bent, back angled forward, he drew my eyes right where they were ashamed to go.

Soon it was our turn to bat. Six wickets down and chasing fifty-seven, the team sent me. Salim stood at the non-striker's end. "Take a single, rotate the strike." Even his shout sounded regal.

The tall, fast bowler sensed my fear and urged the fielders to draw closer. He took a long run up and hurled the ball. I swung and missed.

Salim came over. "What's your name again?" he asked.

"Arun," I said.

Look, Arun, swing the bat low and run, I expected him to say.

"Do you have ten rupees? I forgot my wallet. I'll give it back next week."

I nodded and gazed around, letting people think we were having a tactical discussion.

Salim looked eager, and so I put my hands in my pockets. I made a show of looking, even though I knew I didn't have any money. I curled out my lower lip—nothing. He shrugged and strolled back to the non-striker's end.

The ball came and I swung the bat. We ran, and Salim took the strike. The bowler spat on the ball and rubbed it against his crotch. He took an even longer run up and bowled. *Thwack!* The ball flew beyond the compound wall for a six. Salim held his hand against his eyebrows, and in the shadow cast on his face, I saw the hint of a smile. We won the match with two overs to spare.

I saw him at the vegetable market the next day. I waved at him, but he was busy flirting with the fruit-seller lady. I stared at him for a good minute, until he turned around and lifted his eyebrows, another flicker of recognition. He held guavas in his arms, and his eyes traveled to the person next to me, my mother, and stayed there—perhaps trying to ascertain if the woman next to me was my mother. I tried to interrupt Mother to introduce her to Salim, but by the time she'd turned toward me, he'd walked away, juggling guavas in the air. I wouldn't see him again until a few days later. And we wouldn't be friends until a month after that. But I was already in love with his swagger, something I knew I'd never have.

Our friendship began at an AA meeting meant for our fathers. The air outside the municipality building was hot and sober. Families sat in rows of plastic chairs extending past the veranda. Father stared at Mother. This was what he had to endure, his face said. Mother watched him with fear in her eyes. I'd had enough of their drama.

I scanned the crowd and saw Salim in the last row. He sat next to his father; they had the same chin. At first, I wanted to hide, to not let him see me. Then I sidled up to him; I had never seen anyone I knew at the meetings before.

Salim looked stunned. We exchanged hellos.

"Why didn't you come to the game?" he asked.

"Busy," I said. The truth: I hadn't been invited; the other boys invited me only when they needed an extra fielder.

"Let's get ice cream," Salim said.

We walked over to the ice cream vendor sitting under the shade of the banyan tree, cooling himself with a paper fan. He opened the cart's hatch and inserted his hand into it. Out came two ice cream sticks, one yellow and one pink. I paid.

"Your father drinks?" Salim bit off a chunk of ice.

"That's putting it mildly."

Salim laughed, and my chest expanded.

"What does he do?"

Father spent most of his time away from home in a cargo ship that went back and forth between Maldives and India.

"Sailor? How?"

I was tired of the question. But people were always amazed that somebody in Karimnagar, a thousand kilometers away from the sea, had become a sailor. I told him the story. Years ago, on one particularly tense night at home, our extended family chastised Father for being lazy and unemployed. He stormed out in anger and boarded the Bombay train to find a job and prove them all wrong. By the time the train rolled into Bombay, a full twenty hours later, his tongue was so dry he had to seek a watering hole. That accomplished, he woke up in a cargo ship several miles away from land. Upon discovering an unlabeled, unpackaged, and disoriented entity in the ship, the captain put him to work. As long as he worked, no one cared if he drank, and that was it for him. "So," people usually exclaim on hearing the story, "he did find a job that suited him." But it was only a job, and when he came back home, he drank and called Mother a whore, a randi. Sometimes he'd ask me to dance, but his smell was nauseating. I'd refuse to entertain him, and he'd slap me till my gums bled. I didn't tell Salim any of that, though; I didn't think it'd be cool to do so. But Salim sensed something. "You okay?" he asked.

I nodded and looked at my feet.

He patted my wrist, and a coolness spread across my arm.

For the first time ever, I was sad when the AA meeting was over. I waved goodbye to Salim and went home, the lingering starchiness of the ice stick on my tongue.

Days drifted past, not unlike the way clouds made their way across the sky, this movement in time, some mysterious design under way. August rains downed summer heat. The ice cream vendor disappeared. AA meetings were suspended due to a lack of roofed seating space. The playground turned into a pond, complete with ducks, frogs, and paper boats, and the vegetable market into an assortment of vendors with moving carts, blue tarpaulins, and flexible schedules. Father left, and school resumed. A boy in my class quit. Salim stayed.

The cricket group disbanded into separate units, and our unit was persistent enough to play in the minutes untouched by the evening rain. Salim and I, regulars in this group, met by the adda and waited for the rest. By now, the boys had changed their opinion of me. I was no longer the nerdy kid who couldn't play well; I had important friends. We sat cross-legged, leaning against each other, and talked shit about girls. Someone brought up careers. One boy wanted to serve. "The army will send you back in a box," we said. Another said he'd start a store. "Good luck with that, we'll be your customers"—we made the sign for no money.

Salim said he wanted to be an actor.

"You want to be a Bollywood star?" I asked.

"I am a Khan," he said, and the boys laughed.

"You need English for that." I stretched my legs. I'd seen interviews of Bollywood stars on TV, and they all spoke excellent English.

"English to act in Hindi movies?" Salim chuckled, and the boys laughed at me. I let them. None of us spoke English well enough for movies.

The rain stopped, and we threw the ball around, but mud stuck to it and spattered a boy in the face. We gave up, and Salim and I left the adda.

"Teach me English and I'll teach you how to bat," Salim said, on the way back to our respective homes.

"Who said I don't know batting?"

Salim laughed, a hearty laugh that jumped out of his throat.

"I don't know English well." I was thrilled with the idea that I knew something he didn't.

"You know more than any of the other boys; I heard them say you won a prize in school."

"Only because everybody else was worse."

"Teach me." Salim held my wrist.

Warmth gripped my body. "Right now?" I said.

Salim nodded, and somewhere in my arteries, I knew this was dangerous. But something had been set in motion and I was determined to see it through to its logical conclusion. As we turned the corner and walked up the street, my eyes fell on the house next to ours. Our neighbors liked to spy on us, but no one was there, so far as I could see. Just Chachi's red saree, hung up to dry, fluttered in the wind.

I creaked our gate open. It was just another two-bedroom house, identical in construction to others in the street, with cemented floors and circular stairs built like a garland, leading to the terrace. The house looked normal, but the walls seemed to betray the drama. Melancholy seeped through them. I wondered if Salim could tell.

"I've heard so much about you," Mother said once we were inside. She offered Salim a glass of lemonade.

Salim gave a coy smile. I looked at Mother, her hair tied in a bun, waiting for our empty glasses, a wide smile on her face. She liked him. Why wouldn't she? She probably thought my schoolwork would improve, that I was learning from an older boy.

We left the kitchen, and I showed Salim my prized possession—a globe I'd won in school—and my favorite spot, the terrace. From there I could see that Chachi was peering at us from behind her sari.

She'd be scandalized that I'd brought home a Muslim. Chacha, her husband and a friend of my father's, often said that Muslims were all Pakistanis. He believed they spawned dozens of kids with the intention of taking over India; he acted as though the country's future depended on his vigil. I avoided him and his wife as much as I could.

Some parts of the terrace had already dried, and Salim sat down at the edge and whistled "My Name Is Joker." I washed my feet at the pump and sat next to him, hung my legs in the air so that water drops fell from my feet, one at a time, onto the potted plant below. Kaali, a stray black cat that hung around our house, strode on the parapet wall. Chacha once said that a single black cat could bring a hundred years of misfortune. He urged

Mother to consult a priest and determine the best possible way to appease the gods.

"What can a black cat do to a house that already has your father in it?" Mother said to me after she nodded Chacha off.

Everything around me conjured memories and experiences I wanted to share with Salim. There was so much to tell, the enormity of this task overwhelmed me. I stayed quiet, vacillating between the desire to share everything and nothing.

Salim raised his eyebrows as if to say, *What's the plan?*

I'd brought my English textbook onto the terrace and placed it now on his lap. He flipped through the pages, exasperation apparent in the curve of his lips. He put the book aside and said he wanted to fast-forward to the part where he spoke English. I told him everything worthwhile took time.

He squeezed my hand.

I looked at the textbook for a minute, not really seeing anything on the page. I put the book aside and watched men burning wood in the distance. Smoke drifted over thatched houses in the eventide sky. Crows didn't caw, dogs didn't bark, people didn't quarrel, and for the longest time, there was silence. It felt like we were in a picture titled *Two Boys on a Terrace*.

Then somewhere, a train sounded its horn. Salim smiled and said he liked the view. The train blew its horn again and it was just your regular train horn, but it sounded a lot like the arrival of happiness. Salim placed his arm around me. I pretended to yawn and leaned my neck against his arm. Like a friend. His armpits smelled like dried rice. I smelled him and I smelled him again and I swore it would be the last time I did—I didn't want to be caught, I sensed it was forbidden, but each time I took a breath of it, time stopped and nothing mattered. My father, my mother, the neighbors, the narrow street—everything was dull and pale in comparison, and I kept breathing until my nostrils, with all their eagerness, became accustomed to his scent and my chest grew heavy. I'd lost it, and I held my breath to ease the weight of that finality, but when I breathed again, there it was, that whiff of intoxication. I held my breath again and again. It came to me that I had been waiting to answer something about myself, and now I knew what it was, and this filled me with anxiety—there'd be days, months to think about what it meant, I told myself, but I could no longer deny it. This new anxiety settled into my being like the smoke that melded into the sky, darkening it bit by bit. But in that moment, leaning on his shoulder, I pushed everything out of my mind and looked at the eventide sky, wide and unblemished, and smiled as if I were being photographed.

"Do you want to go to that English movie?" Salim asked the next day. We'd seen posters for *Pirates of the Caribbean* at the adda.

"Ooh, that's a good way to pick up English," I said, looking at his light stubble.

Salim's smile took on a teasing quality. "Do you have to ask your mother?"

"I don't have to," I said, punching his arm.

I snuck money out of Mother's purse, and we took the long route via the train tracks to avoid being seen by people we knew. The secrecy only increased the thrill I felt in the theater when we rubbed shoulders. We hid our faces in our hands, and when the cinema went dark, we rose in delight. The movie had more action than dialogue, half of which I barely understood. "Pirate" was a new word. We repeated to each other: "Hello, pirate," and "Howdy, pirate."

We watched a number of movies together, and there were

always new things to discover. We learned people called 911 in case of emergencies. Sex before marriage was okay. An alien invasion was always on the horizon. We learned how to style our hair like Brad Pitt's with coconut oil and tooth powder. The movies put Salim in an expansive mood. He'd put his arm around my shoulders and tell me what he would have done differently had he been the hero. I'd nod and then we'd go our separate ways. Often, I'd be the first to say goodbye. I sensed that Salim didn't really want to go home. All I had to do, I thought, was invite him to mine. He'd come. But there was the anxiety, which never left. The question of appropriateness. I couldn't invite him without an excuse; Salim wouldn't be comfortable coming without the excuse.

But one night the excuse presented itself. We had just watched *The Lord of the Rings*. Salim's father was out of town, and Salim said he'd be going back from the movie to an empty home. I felt something stir in my pants.

"I wish the movie kept going," Salim said, his arm around me.

"Until the morning, right?" I said.

Salim turned toward me. "What?"

"Because you're so scared of staying by yourself in the dark." I laughed.

He held me by the neck and tickled me in the ribs. "My *precious*."

I wrenched free and ran a few feet ahead. "Do you want to sleep at my place tonight?"

"Will your mother be okay with that?"

"Come with me," I said, wishing the night would never end.

At home Mother okayed my proposition as I knew she would and brought out the extra sheets. I made his bed, next to mine on the floor. Salim wanted to shower. I opened the bathroom for him and pressed a towel in his hands. I tucked my hardness between my legs and hoped it wouldn't show through my underwear. Salim came back from the bathroom in the towel, naked from the waist up. His body emanated heat, but it was my face that felt warm as I hovered around him, asking if he needed another towel. He had hair all over his chest, a mole on his biceps. I had one in the exact same place.

I gave him one of Father's shirts and ran to the bathroom. I couldn't stand it anymore. I pulled down my fly. The scent of him lingered and I stood there inhaling it, watching myself grow. The tap was wet. Salim had been naked right here. I touched the tap. Its long handle could have been his shaft. I stroked it again and again, bathing in the scent he'd left behind. I perched down and took it in my mouth and cocked my head back and forth, imagining him scrunching his face, and I knew this was wrong, something was very wrong with me, but I could not stop, and with each hold of my mouth, I felt my penis grow harder and harder, and I held my hand to the hardness while I continued to move my tongue over the tip of the handle, licking it in each untouched spot, teasing it, closing my mouth around it, working against the handle faster and faster till I came.

By the time I cleaned up and came back, he was fast asleep. I fell on my mattress and lay awake for a long time, torn between wanting to wrap myself around Salim and running away that very night before I got outed.

When I woke up the next morning, Salim had already left, and Mother was searching the house, turning up plastic chairs. She asked me if I'd taken the twenty rupees she'd placed in the folds of a magazine that had been on the teapoy. I hadn't, but I felt my stomach tighten and I saw the same thought cross her eyes. Had Salim stolen the money? I asked if she'd maybe put the money somewhere else and forgotten. She accepted that as a possibility. But I left for school wishing I could make the money appear. I would somehow detect that the wind had swept the note to a corner. Or Mother would remember where she'd misplaced it. Anything really. I knew Salim had money problems—I paid for everything. But I thought he'd ask if he needed something. I sat through class with difficulty and returned home.

Mother said she hadn't found the money. I dropped my bag and went looking for him. I figured I'd ask him casually if he happened to see any money lying on the ground that night. I went to his house, but the gate was locked. I didn't see him the whole week. Mother forgot about the money. Every day after school, I did the circuit. I went to the playground, the theater, the market, the adda. I spun my globe, wondering where he was. I lost interest in school. No one asked me to teach English anymore; no one squeezed my wrist as he did. Each day I looked for him, the money became less and less important. And I slapped my thighs in anger. What I had done with the tap, my sin, had pushed him away. Every time I went to the bathroom, I remembered, and my penis began to expand. I was ashamed; I took a blade, steadied my hand, made a tiny cut. A drop of blood emerged, and the sight of it stopped my shame. I apologized to him, for desiring him, for doubting him.

Then the next week, I came home from school and saw him sitting on the sofa, laughing with Mother as if they were best friends, as if she were the reason he'd come to our house. I went straight to my room and stood by the window. Salim came in and put his hand on my shoulder. He whispered, *"Sorry";* his mouth brushed against my ear.

"I had to go to my father's village. It was an emergency," Salim said.

"What happened?" I asked, still upset.

"My father started drinking again; we had to take him. There, he can drink all the buffalo milk he wants." He grinned.

In spite of myself, I let out a chuckle. "I looked for you everywhere," I said.

"Sorry," he repeated, and enveloped me with his long arms. I turned and hugged him. Locked in his embrace, I looked out the window. A pigeon lay on the neighbors' wall looking for grains. He held me tighter. The pigeon found a grain a couple of feet away on the wall. His hands caressed my back. The pigeon hopped to the grain. He kissed me on the cheek. The pigeon grabbed the grain and flew—not knowing that it lifted into the sky my soul.

Most days, I found Salim at home eating Mother's pakoras, regaling her with all sorts of tales. He'd say that he'd marry a woman like her, making her blush and laugh in a way I'd never seen before, and then he'd turn to me and wink. I thought nothing of it, all it meant was that I didn't have to explain what we were to her. I could linger in the painting Two Boys on the Terrace.

January brought my fourteenth birthday. We bought a bubble stick for laughs, something we'd both done when we were much younger, and rinsed it with soap and blew bubbles at each other, our feet grazing one another as we did. We hadn't proceeded beyond what we'd already done. I hadn't asked if his kiss on the cheek meant more than casual fraternal affection, the kind we saw in Bollywood movies. There was time; we'd get there. But I found myself growing in confidence; I threw away the blade in the bathroom.

Mother baked a cake for my birthday and gave us money for movie tickets. We went to the theater, this time unafraid. Salim copied the gestures of film stars, and I copied him. I cupped my palms around my mouth when I spoke in a low voice, as he did. I drank chai in the evening, as he did. How was I to know things would change so soon?

Chacha beckoned me the day after my birthday and asked me what Salim's name was. He had seen him around the house often and wanted to know who he was. He knew Salim was Muslim and this was his way of confirming. Fucking pig.

"Samir," I said, and ran.

February followed. Father would return any day—it was time. Dark clouds of rain lurched forward in the sky. Shadows the size of mountains cast gloom everywhere. Vendors in the vegetable market packed up their carts in a hurry. The ice cream vendor was nowhere. The playground was desolate. The cinema had a padlock—temporarily closed for projector repair. I found Salim sitting on the train tracks, throwing pebbles at the ties.

"It's only temporary," I said. But I couldn't hide the fear in my voice. Chacha would tell Father, I was sure, and he wouldn't let me see Salim again.

Salim stared at the tracks. "I'm leaving for Bombay," he said. He wanted to try his luck in films. Every pebble echoed a dull cracking noise, again and again.

"When?" I asked. The rumble of clouds silenced everything.

"Soon. I'll come say bye. In a couple of days," he said. He stood up and brushed the dirt from his pants. "There's nothing here. I have to go." He squeezed me on the shoulder and left.

The night Salim was supposed to leave, I woke to the sound of a woman's cries. Cuss words, a chorus of harsh voices. It was past midnight. A thief had been caught, I thought. But then I heard Salim's voice, pleading. I sprang to my feet; he'd come to say goodbye.

I opened the door. I saw that Father had returned, was standing in the hall near the other bedroom. And something was happening. Father was kicking Salim in the stomach, and Salim, shirtless, twisted on the floor. Chacha and Chachi stood watching. It didn't make any sense. Father slapped Mother, crying, semi-dressed, in the face and went back to kicking Salim. Had Salim been caught stealing money? Chachi dragged Mother inside the bedroom.

Father bent down and slapped Salim in the face.

"You circumcised bastard," Chacha's voice boomed.

I didn't understand any of it. "Please don't hit him," I said.

Chacha shoved me, and I fell back into the room. "Stay inside," he shouted, and bolted the door. No matter how much I tried, I couldn't move. My feet wouldn't cooperate. I couldn't open my mouth either. It was as if someone had bound my legs and gagged my mouth. From the floor, I watched the gap between the door and the floor, the light sneaking in, the way it fell on my globe, which for some reason was on the floor too. I couldn't comprehend what I'd seen. Why couldn't I move? It had something to do with what I'd seen in the seconds before Chacha pushed me inside, something to do with Mother appearing not quite herself, I couldn't do anything other than look at the gap. Salim had taken something of what I had, this much I felt. My body shook and shook on the cold floor of my room.

An hour passed and the voices dissolved into silence. My body returned to me. I got up and ran away from home.

·   ·   ·

I never saw Salim again or went to Karimnagar after that. For a while, I worked at a dhaba in Odisha, several hundred kilometers away. The dhaba sat next to the highway and attracted a fair amount of dust and flies. A stray dog slept under the tables and I'd feed it leftovers. The work itself wasn't bad. I'd serve food to customers and scrub their plates. Nights were the busiest and afternoons the quietest. Some afternoons, when I was dusting the dhaba signboard or picking at a solitary grain of rice lodged inside the stove, I'd think of Salim and I'd briefly wonder what happened that night. Before I could arrive at an answer, I'd feel a sharp pain deep within my chest, and I'd distract myself with one task or another. Occasionally, a customer would complain about flies and I'd take a grayed tablecloth and swish at them. But the flies were also like memories. They had a mind of their own, they flew out of reach and returned uninvited; they'd entice, gently whirring in the air, nasty little fuckers.

I tried to forget him. Tried to forget my last night at home, how I'd raised myself from the floor an hour after the house fell quiet. Found the door unlocked and stepped into the hallway. There was no one. I'd walked past the other bedroom, which remained closed, and felt sick. I limped outside; there was complete darkness. Kaali emerged from the black of the night and meowed at me. "Come with me," I'd said to the cat. My knees wobbled. A song played in my head—the song Salim used to whistle. "My Name Is Joker." I danced past the veranda. One step at a time, I shook my legs. Past the house, past the playground, past the adda, past the vegetable market, past the train tracks, past the movie theater, past the places he'd become a part of, past me.

The Immigrant

The long wait in the cold white hall alarmed Aditya. He held the document folder to his chest like he desired nothing more than its safety, like he wanted the authorities to know that he'd worked toward these documents; they were evidence that he could do the right thing, proof that he was normal, an ordinary immigrant, could be given a chance.

The blue-jacketed Homeland Security man overseeing the line strode back and forth repeating in a loud, hoarse voice, Please have your passport and arrival form ready. It had been two hours, and the line had barely inched closer to the series of glass enclosures where uniformed officers interviewed the arrivals, making people put their paws on a black box of sorts. There were quite a few immigration officers, each taking their time, each a cold, clinical inspector of mongrels. If people were nervous, they weren't saying much; the line remained quiet, and Aditya was sure that if this were back home, all lines would have collapsed, and there would be strangers on either side of him and they'd inquire about his family and where they came from and what properties they had.

He could not imagine telling anybody the truth: he came from a family of broke Marxists, he'd rather starve than rabidly acquire properties, and he stood in line because his mother needed a lung transplant. It was his choice to come to the States, an idea that had steadily taken hold after learning how much he could earn. At the airport, when he was leaving India, his mother had implored him to stay. His father looked away when she spoke, as she repeated again and again that she'd be fine, he should stay, they would figure it out, find a way through their debt, don't go. But he had seen too much, all his life; he knew what they could and couldn't figure out, and he had to do something about it.

The plan was simple. He'd get a master's degree as quickly as possible from whichever place took him, find a well-paying tech job, and send money home. In the end there had been only one program that accepted him and only one Indian bank that let him take out a student loan without an asset guarantee, and he flew with the tuition money order and $600 in cash. He expected to share a room with someone and pay $300 in rent and $300 for the security deposit, which left nothing for food until he could support himself.

Keep your passport and arrival form on top, the blue-jacketed man shouted again, looking at his watch and back at the line. Aditya leafed through his passport: the inside cover, his photo, his home address, his date of birth, the insignia, the empty pages. The blue-jacketed man stopped next to him, watching a spate of new arrivals join the line, making it longer and longer, and miraculously clipped open a path to the short line for citizens. Aditya ran there, triumphant.

There was a white officer interviewing travelers ten feet from where he stood. Up close, the black box became a fingerprint scanner, and he could see the officer speaking with an elderly woman, gesturing toward what must be a camera. Soon, it'd be his turn. If a photograph was what the officer wanted, he had several in his document folder, old passport-sized photos that he'd brought exactly for a moment like this, but no, they wouldn't accept it, he didn't think so, what they required was a picture in the moment, something that said, *This is the face you wore on the day you were let into this country,* something that said, *I submit.* Never do a thing you are ashamed of, his father had always said, and here he was—*Take it, take these documents too, stamp me. Let me in.*

Outside the terminal, it was dark. Cars lined up, shooting beams of light, swerving around, grabbing adults and kids, moving strangely, inexorably. He found it exhilarating. Goose bumps flared on his arm, the air crackling with possibilities, or so he felt until a mild breeze caught his face and he realized he was merely cold. The month was still August, the last days of it, but a note of winter already whistled in the wind.

A short man with a broad chest walked toward him holding a printout. Aditya had emailed his flight information to PISA, the Indian student association at the university, and was told that someone would pick him up and give him temporary accommodation for a few days. This someone was Ratnakar; they shook hands. Welcome to Philadelphia, Ratnakar said. He said he recognized Aditya from his Facebook page. Aditya found this both impressive and creepy. He'd used flowers and mountains as profile pictures. There was just one picture of him on the site—you'd have to hike past several mountains before getting to it.

Ratnakar stared at a curly-haired man with a cart bearing three suitcases. That, he said, was Mani. He approached Mani in the same manner as he'd approached Aditya.

Things moved quickly. Mani said he was super excited, he

was in the same program as Aditya, he couldn't imagine choosing anything other than AI, it was 2010 after all, AI was the future. He hadn't found housing because, like Aditya, he'd been warned by PISA in a superlong email not to sign a lease without comparing rental prices, without seeing the apartment first, and did they think it'd take superlong to find a place?

Aditya knew nothing and so he processed everything: Ratnakar called Gagan, a PhD student in immunology, and asked him to come to the curb; he was waiting in something called a cell phone lot; the weather would get colder in October; there wasn't much to do in the winter months unless you wanted to go ice-skating and break your arm; what made Ratnakar happy, according to him, was helping out freshers like Aditya and Mani; the idea behind PISA was for students to pay it forward; the car was small, the only way everything would fit was if they sat down and had Ratnakar stack some of the suitcases on their laps; white people were not friendly like desi, you had to be chill and earn their trust over time; there were things one shouldn't do in this country; plagiarism was a strict no-no; seat belts were compulsory. All these lexicons, he was like a sand particle on a beach, wave after wave rushing at him—there was so much to observe so much to hear so much to know it felt impossible to be still.

The suitcases blocked everything. He couldn't see Ratnakar or Gagan or the streets; the underside of his wrist held the blue rim of one of the suitcases just inches from his eyes. The little he saw gave him no pleasure. To the left, a sliver of road, speeding cars. To the right, Mani similarly straining, holding a conversation with Ratnakar on where they each had relatives in the States, taking in Ratnakar's wisdom on life here.

None of what Ratnakar said made sense. There wasn't

anything incomprehensible in what he said, this being a different country, but the mere suggestion of there being an etiquette, an entire system of evaluation that he couldn't immediately parse, bothered Aditya. It was there in the way Ratnakar told them they should never eat with their hands in public; it was there in the way he told them not to sit next to a white person without wearing copious amounts of deodorant; it was there in the clean pressed air that came in through the little gap in the window. For a second, he had the feeling that this was not the United States he'd come to but the home of some kind of monster that preyed on people. The seniors knew what it could do, but the freshers didn't, which was why they were being smuggled away to safety, away from the creature that would attack them, and for that he felt grateful. But then it struck him that these men were already maimed. How else could they know what they knew? Why else would they offer such definitive instructions? Was there no way to escape?

The car slowed to a stop. They dragged the suitcases into the dark, past a building door propped open with a red brick, past mailboxes, and stopped in front of the stairs. Gagan lived somewhere else, and Ratnakar had gone with him for a quick smoke, telling them to go inside. The tenants were all either Indian or Chinese; Ratnakar's name was on the label for 3A. Mani seemed astonished by the weight of his own suitcases. Packed by his mother, he said, with all kinds of eatables. Aditya remembered his own mother's efforts to pack. She had wanted to make a variety of snacks, had been so excited to cook that she'd sent him and his father to buy three different kinds of flour, but by the time they returned, she was on the kitchen floor wheezing so hard she'd begun to sob. After she recovered, he'd made her promise not to cook, told her it was for the best, he didn't want to get fat anyway.

On the second floor, Ratnakar overtook them and ran into a Chinese student taking out the trash. They nodded at each other and said hi. Aditya asked Ratnakar if they were friends, the Chinese student and him, but no, they never spoke, they simply said hi to each other from time to time. This was a thing people did.

The apartment door opened to the smell of curry long made. All the lights were out, people already sleeping, five in all, two in each bedroom, one in the living room, and when they quietly rolled in the suitcases, there wasn't enough space for Aditya and Mani to spread a bedsheet and sleep on the floor. One of them would have to squeeze between the suitcases, and the other would have to sleep in the kitchen. It was clear that no one had been cooking; the kitchen was forlorn, the smell of masala everywhere, something of its vitality gone, dulled, a past baked into the fabric of the air.

Aditya ignored the hunger in his stomach, swept away crumbs on the kitchen floor, and spread a bedsheet. Having journeyed for more than twenty-six hours, he needed a shower, but Mani had gone to the bathroom first. He sat on the sheet, and his eyes fell upon the series of cabinets. He stared at them lying down, and his eyes began to droop; wrist underneath his head, he saw knobs round as Earth, doors wide as suitcases, and hidden inside were oceans of sleep.

He woke up, wrist limp from the weight of his head and the apartment still dark. He didn't want to disturb others, tried falling asleep again, counting sheep, a thousand of them, but they migrated too, switching places, bleating here and there, forcing him to start over. He sat up. He calculated that it was noon back home. Making a phone call was out of the question, too expensive. He'd promised to send an email to his father once he'd arrived, confirming that all was good. In the morning, he'd ask to borrow a laptop. He pictured his father going to the internet café, handing someone a slip with an email address and password, requesting they type up a short question: *Arrived?* He saw it so clearly: his father waiting in the café with the slip he had written, stooping in the narrow walkway, lost, trying to identify a sympathetic soul who'd take the slip, hometown men in tiny cubicles all around him, looking at their monitors. Aditya couldn't help but insert himself in the moment: he put his arm around his father's neck and turned him homeward, as though there was no longer a need for the slip or for any of it, laughing at his father's elation, exiting the café, walking hand in hand.

He got up and made his way to the bathroom, past Mani, who he saw had used a textbook for a pillow. In the bathroom, he examined the assortment of products lying on the counter: a couple of lotions, shaving creams, mouthwash, toothpaste. All brands new to him except the toothpaste. Sitting on the toilet, he read through the ingredients listed on all the products he could reach with his hand, their histories complex. It did not matter at all that he didn't understand them; reading them gave him pleasure. When he was done, he looked for the bidet, but there was none. No tap or mug either. Behind the shower curtain, tucked inside the tub, there was nothing. He discovered the presence of a paper roll next to his knee and its utility struck him. He wiped his bottom with it and felt deeply unclean. Like he could not be sure that there weren't any little pieces of paper stuck down there. What unhygienic nonsense; he had to shower right away. He stole toward his suitcase and retrieved a towel and jumped in the shower. Only after he had water pouring all over his body, after he had scrubbed himself clean, did he feel at peace. But a momentary peace; he'd thrown the shower curtain outside the tub earlier, and there was now a substantial pool of water on the bathroom floor. He hadn't encountered a shower curtain before; he felt defeated, like he couldn't understand the first thing about anything. He stepped into the pool and grabbed the paper roll and got to work, hoping the others wouldn't find out what he had done, that there wouldn't be much more for him to learn, that the fucking roll would last.

Morning cut through the living room window. Bars of light he could almost eat, particles dancing in felt heat. He and Mani made their way down the stairs. Everything seemed different. The carpet in the hallway, which he'd taken to be blue, was actually sea green. Something about the location of the mailboxes had changed overnight, their distance from the door no longer awkward, the boxes themselves not as shabby as he'd first thought them, the sun having made the building rosier. Outside, Mani exclaimed at every upscale car on the street. Aditya felt it was silly to covet fancy cars, even outrageous when so many people had nothing to eat, but it wasn't his place to say and they were in a whole new world now, and so he smiled at Mani and took pictures on his flip phone, to capture as much as possible of the country, parked cars and magnolia trees, streetlights and traffic cones, clean roads and green yards, red bricks and white lettering, everything bathed in brightness, the whole landscape sparkling, shining, screaming this was the vastness he had expected to see, this was America. He could touch it.

The housing companies were firm, they had nothing available until January. Except for a three-bedroom house that would cost $2,000 a month. It was generally possible to secure an apartment after arriving, but the university had accepted more students than the year before and there was a bit of a shortage. Aditya couldn't believe it. If PISA had warned him that this was a possibility, he'd have arrived a little earlier. Although how he'd have been able to afford food, he didn't know. He hadn't had anything all day except for the homemade sweets Mani had shared.

They roamed the streets dialing the numbers on rental signs. He found the concept of voice mail discomfiting. Babbling into a flip phone with no one on the other end—it was as though a tiny part of him had been cleaved, separated from his body, and thrown into the speaker, possibly discarded; all the same, he left messages explaining who he was and what he was looking for, would they please get back to him?

He got a call back from one. He'd spoken as clearly as he could, but the man on the other end said he couldn't understand which building Aditya had called about, and Aditya told him it was the one on Spruce Street, but the man kept saying, What? What? What? He'd never heard of that street and he'd been living in the city all his life. When Aditya finally spelled it out, the man said, Oh, you mean Spruce Street! That unit is long gone.

They continued, their shadows gliding on the sidewalk, slanting into storefronts, flitting from store to store like avid shoppers. Aditya thought it funny that it was only their second day in the country and capitalism already had their shadows enthralled.

Mani wasn't in the mood for any humor, his face thin and gaunt from exhaustion. The sun formed little stars on the dashboards of parked cars, which no longer impressed him. Instead, he stood outside Chipotle, his head on the restaurant glass, pondering. He wanted a burrito, he said; he'd heard about them from his cousins—would Aditya go to Chipotle with him?

Aditya felt tested, the rabble in his stomach imploring him. But the money he had was for housing, so no, he couldn't; he said his stomach wasn't feeling great. They emerged from the restaurant minutes later, Mani holding a to-go bag and Aditya breathing out his shadow.

After four days of search, they'd still found nothing. Aditya collapsed on a park bench, tired and alone. His back hurt from sleeping on the hard floor. He hadn't done anything adventurous, but somehow there was a rip in his right shoe. He'd left the apartment to get dinner, the excuse he'd given Mani because he couldn't keep accepting the eatables Mani offered. He was too proud and also couldn't bring himself to continue depriving Mani of the food his mother lovingly had packed for him.

He'd applied for part-time jobs around campus and hadn't heard back about anything. And Ratnakar was of little use, playing Xbox and smoking with his pals all day, suggesting Aditya and Mani rent the three-bedroom house and move there as quickly as possible, giving them tips on restaurants to eat at. But the best burgers around were none of Aditya's business; he hadn't had a meal in four days, his stomach a liquid racket and his head a dizzy ball, and when Ratnakar's roommate told him that this park had the best sunsets, that he should check it out because you could smash a serve at the dipping sun and enjoy a cold beer and what could be better, Aditya nodded and left right away, as though he were determined not to miss it, as though dinner were the least of his concerns.

A strong wind lifted his head, the scent of honeysuckle and mulch in his face. Skyscrapers turned orange as though lit by fire. The buzz of a bee; he waved his hands in the air. Orphaned shouts, faint cars, the skitter of leaves, the quack of a duck, the slam of a tennis ball across the court, all in his ear newly freed from self-pity. A beagle barked. He watched it chase a duck and flee from it. September was here. The beagle ran back to a woman with a stroller. A flutter of moths. They walked toward the bench, the mother and the dog. He wondered if his mother still went on a walk every evening, now that he couldn't join her anymore.

He nodded at the woman; this was now a thing he did.

On orientation day rain lashed hard on the streets. He arrived late, drenched, his hair flattened, his shoes full of water. He had no umbrella. You got caught real bad, the administrator said. Behind her, he saw a spread: fruits, chocolates, cookies?

He dashed to the restroom, where he marveled at the drier pulling water from his hair, and hurried out, his shoes leaving a trail of puddles in the wake of every step he took. The administrator blocked his path to the spread. Aditya introduced himself, pronouncing his name thrice.

She held a stack of cards for students in the program. He watched her unroll the band holding the cards together and look through the photographs. She paused briefly to inspect every other card, humming apologies—This one, no, not this one either—his make of face confusing in the wad of brown. No worries, he said, helping her pick. There! The card made it real, his name attached to an institution and purified by association, the pleasure of credibility on his neck. He wiped off a raindrop that had fallen onto the card, his chin still leaking. He imagined telling his father that he could swipe it on a bus. What impressed him most was its sleekness, the card thin and sharp like it could cut through space. All he had to do was show it.

By the time he got to the food, there was no line to cut through. It was too late. An inventory of what was left: a grape, two pretzels, popcorn kernels, tissue paper.

The apartment he finally found was tiny, a studio thirty minutes from school. It was in a neighborhood they hadn't looked in before, with more Black people than in the ones they'd been originally looking at. He briefly wondered if Mani would be scared—he'd seen him flinch when a Black homeless man had approached them near Chipotle—but that was no reason to give up on a perfectly good apartment. It had yellow walls, casement windows, and a little nook for a kitchen. How much was the rent? Anna, the owner, an Ethiopian immigrant, said $550. That would leave him fifty dollars for food. Aditya smiled and immediately regretted it—if he'd had any bargaining leverage it was gone with the smile. Anna said that she had multiple people interested, but she liked him; he too was from somewhere else. Then she chuckled, a laugh much like his mother's. His heart sank.

He steadied himself and took out the flip phone. Mani's

voice jumped out of the phone when Aditya called him with the news. He said that was wonderful and that Aditya should tell Anna they were taking it. And oh, they'd celebrate at Chipotle, because why not.

Aditya left the unit with the lease agreement they needed to sign and return with copies of their passports. The cloudless sky gleamed azure. Later in Chipotle: a seven-dollar meal, the sum of five meals back home, food translated into money; if conversion was at the heart of all things pure, the first bite of burrito sank into his mouth like pieces of sky falling down his face, each gulp an explosion of color.

That evening he went to the computer lab to make copies of their passports for the lease. Mani shuffled a few feet away, speaking with his mother, the conversation a joyous aria. Aditya sat behind a computer. Calling cards existed only in multiples of ten, the lowest value costing ten dollars; *America is good but very expensive,* he wrote to his father. He imagined his father carrying this information home, weighing the distance traveled, unpacking every word. He was there at home: his father's tattered slippers outside their apartment door, his mother's brown handbag next to the sofa, the stupid magnet on their fridge, the curved handle on their kitchen chair; he tried to hear what his parents were saying, but nothing came.

Someday, he'd make a phone call.

You're too naive, Ratnakar said later, when he told him where the apartment was. Get your head out of the clouds. The neighborhood isn't safe. He didn't need to see the street; he knew it was full of criminals, and if Aditya couldn't see that, it was because he was too impractical. Mani moved his head a little in either direction, as though caught between two valid perspectives, but finally agreed with Ratnakar, said that he didn't want to live in a Black neighborhood.

Aditya was furious and waved the lease at them. He'd promised Anna that he'd return with Mani's signature, passport copies, the security deposit and first month's rent; she'd trusted him. I gave her my word, he said. They were being absurd. A big part of your fear is actually stupidity, Aditya told them. He held back from saying too that it was racist.

Ratnakar said he couldn't just sit back and let something bad happen to them; he was just trying to help because he knew these things, they didn't. Mani asked Ratnakar where else they could live.

Take the three-bedroom and find more roommates over time, Ratnakar said, as though exasperated that the simplest solution was beyond them. Mani turned to Aditya somewhat sheepishly and said that he didn't want to live near Black people, that he'd rather pay more than live somewhere unsafe. Aditya couldn't stand it; these were the people he'd room with? How could they think like that? How were they not ashamed of themselves?

I can't afford it, Aditya said, and left the apartment with his suitcase.

At the bottom of the stairs, Mani asked him to return, to apologize. We'll figure it out tomorrow, he said. It was super late, where would Aditya even find to stay this late? He pulled at Aditya's hand, urging him to come back in.

He moved a little and the stair creaked. The muffled soundtrack of a TV snuck into his ear. A cat began meowing in one of the apartments and he couldn't listen anymore. He looked into Mani's eyes and said, I'm sorry, I don't have any money.

. . .

In the bus shelter, he sat shaking. He leaned against a burger advertisement and kept his feet on the suitcase; he'd wait out the cold night. When morning came, he'd roll his suitcase to Anna's and ask if she'd let him rent without a security deposit, failing which he'd ask around for help. Any help. He pulled out a bedsheet and wrapped it around his chest. Had he been too hasty? Could he have not said anything and left the apartment in the morning? The whiz of a bug around his ear. How loud were these crickets, how bright was that moon, how tolerant the air; what gave this country his fucking salvation? The shaking gradually stopped. He tried sleeping. It wouldn't come. He gazed at the flower print on the bedsheet; his mother had found the strength to accompany him shopping and picked it for its warm hues. He pictured her standing at the kitchen sink, looking out the window as she often did, finding something interesting, like the bloom of a wild hyacinth or the maw of a cloud. How could he ever let her down?

The occasional car drove past. He slid lower, anchoring himself in the now.

The dance of lights far ahead, a police car hovering.

Fuck, what story would he tell them? If they asked, the answer to all queries: Everything was golden. Motto for life.

He peered into the night.

Morning came and left. Anna said no, the housing office said no, the wheels on his suitcase said no. As with the job hunt. Legally, he was not allowed to work outside designated university offices on campus, but he'd moved past that fear and inquired at gas stations, laundromats, diners, the establishments that paid in cash. They all turned him away.

The sun burned his back, and he sat under a tree, hot and crisp. He had no water. Suitcase next to his arm, he felt like a hawker selling bangles under the shade. Dozens of students crisscrossed the campus, the excitement of a new beginning caught in the wild. He felt the air move through the open space. Laughter and birdsong sat alike, heat merging into sound. He slept with a hand on his wares, legs on the grass, and the pull of a bicycle in his dreams. Soon, it was dark and there were enough bug bites on his arms to keep him scratching for a while. Students roamed the pathways illuminated by lights. It was too late; he'd figure something out the next day.

The fluorescent glow of campus police alerted him. He left the suitcase behind the tree, in the dark where it would not be seen. The smell of pizza carried over, somebody's takeout. He walked a few steps toward the library, where he could pee and get some water. Something had changed, his pants held him from walking properly, they were sliding down. He tightened his belt to the last hole and marched with more ease.

He checked the suitcase. He hadn't gone far, he'd been keeping watch most of the time, but he had to make sure nobody touched it. They were all in there—books, clothes, and toiletries. He layered up as if he knew it would be a long night. He was ready for the dark moments; if there was to be light at the end, he'd be there to catch it, to let it sink into him. Right away, abdominal pain. Crouching down with cramps, he lay on his sheet. Somebody had left a half-eaten apple on a bench and he'd grabbed it earlier. He took a little bite and spat out mushy green. It tasted rotten. Water, his best friend. He drifted in and out of consciousness, his father's voice stirring in his ears, the chaos of daybreak, light blinding his eyes shut. When he woke up, a campus police officer stood in front of him. He stuttered something about waiting for a friend. The officer said he was not allowed to camp there, and sweat pooled down his back. He dragged the suitcase to the engineering school building.

Flyers on the bulletin board. He felt dizzy, he needed water, he tottered through the corridor and drank from the fountain. Splashing some on his face, he gasped. Where had he left his suitcase? All the way back. He shuffled there, arm to the wall. Near the board, he ran into Mani speaking on the phone.

There was a flyer: ROOMMATE NEEDED. Martin (Yuchen) was the guy's name; he had a spare bedroom for $600 in a good neighborhood close to the university. Mani was taking it; he'd find a roommate to bring down the rent later. He asked Aditya where he'd slept the past two nights. I told you to stay, he said with a blank stare.

Aditya said nothing; he felt weak. Like he couldn't will it any longer. I'm sorry, he said. Can I room with you? He stared at the window that lit the corridor, and the disappointment on Anna's face when he'd said sorry came back to him.

Shame dipped from his eyebrows, sweat all over the move.

Light vanished in the new apartment after noon. He took a couple of biscuits from the packet Mani offered and spread his sheet opposite the corner Mani had chosen. They had no furniture. Someone had told Mani that people left stuff on certain street corners, so they trawled the streets for abandoned furniture. A treasure hunt for the brightest lamp in the world. Sifting through the remains, they pocketed a pair of scissors. What else was available? A broken chair. Cardboard boxes. Some pencils. Farther away, a mattress. It wouldn't work—Mani feared bedbugs. He'd rather purchase a new mattress that would stand the test of time. Would Aditya help him carry it from the mattress store on Walnut Street? Would Aditya later accompany him to the grocery store? Would Aditya . . . The answer for all future questions: Yes.

Heaving the mattress into the dark room, he reached for the switch.

Ten days since he had landed. He hadn't found a job yet. He needed to hold up his end of the bargain, make his share of the rent. Sirens blazed through the street, fire engines heading somewhere. The library beckoned, but he stayed rooted to the ground, watching. Jesus, move, a guy behind him on the sidewalk said.

One moment, said the help-desk guy at the library, pulling up the employment application system. What was his last name again? He opened his mouth to respond, to spell. Instead, he produced it, the card sliding out of his wallet the easiest thing in the world, his voice disappearing on himself. No remained the answer, there was already an existing application with this name. He had already applied, there were no jobs available at the moment, he was a fool to make the guy think it a new application, what a waste of time, the look on the librarian's face said it all.

Classes whizzed past him, his head full of syntax and jargon. Half the things he heard eluded him as though he were a kindergartner sitting in on an advanced math class, the graphical representations drawn on the whiteboard catching his interest the most. Words like "kernel," "forest," and "python" began to mean something other than what he knew. Students scribbled furiously and solved math problems that sounded like static coming through a speaker. The professors were kind, they directed him to texts that illustrated the basic concepts, all of which were rudimentary to most others in the class, who'd stopped answering his questions after a certain point, Mani among them, he had to finish his assignment first. Who could blame him? The computer science education Aditya received back home was directly proportional to the number of words strewn on his degree certificate, desperation pushing him this far, what disease struck his mind he didn't know, the simplest of tasks lay beyond his grasp, buttoning his shirt took five minutes, lurking around a department event for a pizza slice the cause of much affliction, talking to a white person left his armpits waterlogged, the amount of effort it took to form sentences in his head nothing short of extraordinary, all the basic responses hidden deep in his head like rockets whose launch buttons had to be painstakingly assembled on request, and he began forgetting things, first he forgot to lock the apartment and ran back afraid only to realize he had locked it, next he forgot hours, he found himself jumping from one moment in time to another without much of a consciousness in between, he had no idea what he'd done the day before, the present the only place he could be, all other time disappearing beneath his feet. After a while there was nobody to blame for this malaise but himself. Except one thing, the rent he needed to make—he could lay that on capitalism. He burst into uncontrollable laughter, flailing his arms like a child, dark humor his new best friend. He made himself go to the park, to catch himself.

At the park, he took out the sugar crystals he'd stolen from the department kitchen and rolled them on his tongue. He'd done this a few times, and every time it had worked beautifully, hunger staved off for a minute. A magic trick, a diversion. He sat watching the beagle and the mother with the stroller once again, closer. Squirrels skipped around with nuts in their hands. The mother stopped to check on her baby in the stroller, and the dog strained against the leash. Toby, stop, said the woman. Sit, she said, and the beagle reluctantly sat down. The woman smiled at her baby. Say Mommy, she requested of the baby. Toby barked at Aditya, and the mother caught him looking at them. He walked away. On the way home, he stopped outside a Mongolian restaurant. A board caught his eye: HELP WANTED, $9/HR.

The clap of knives, laughter all around in the kitchen of the Mongolian restaurant. There was relief in the air after a false alarm concerning an ICE officer who might have entered the restaurant, and his colleagues were freely swapping stories over the grill, how they'd found their first job in the country, how quickly everything could fall apart. Nargie said he sucked a delicious little cock at this gas station in the South. Jose said he slept outside a strawberry farm until they took him. Some grandma asked Pedro if he'd mow the lawn for her. Aditya said it was the dog. He hadn't found anything until Toby the dog barked at him and made him leave the park in time, how lucky was that; everybody found this hilarious. It's true, he said.

He chopped onions the way his mother had taught him, rapid incisive movements along the axis, taking pleasure in the eight-inch Wüsthof, a knife sharp enough to slice through anything. Accidentally his finger. Blood gushed on the onions. Pedro tore a kitchen cloth and told him to wrap it tight. Nargie said it took time to get used to the knives here. Jose agreed. It's inevitable, kiddo, he said.

Go back to your own country, a man yelled from the sidewalk. Aditya kept walking, hugging his chest, shivering a little. Entering the apartment building, he freed his arms; he'd need a coat. Martin met him at the door, and they had a decent conversation. Aditya found himself stuttering, reaching for words, but Martin remained patient and willing to listen, like he had been the few times they'd gotten a chance to talk. That freed him a little. He told him about the thing his professor said in class, how the field was advanced enough to give intelligent speech to a robot, how if you equipped a dog with that sort of AI, it'd bark all sorts of useful data.

In his room, Martin spun the globe on his desk and pointed out his hometown: Nanjing. Where's yours? he asked Aditya.

You won't find it here, Aditya said. He thrust his index finger between two cities in the southern part of India. Somewhere here.

He looked at the room strewn with books, at the swivel chair where Martin sat, bending forward. An idea: he'd barely saved enough for a coat; could he later ask Martin to lend him the difference? Martin read the names of Indian cities as if he were trying to memorize them once and for all. Suddenly, he turned toward Aditya and said, Do you miss it?

Aditya looked at him.

Home, do you miss it? Martin said.

A simple question, but the longer he thought about it, the

more impossible it seemed to answer. Intellectually, yes, he did miss home, but also, he could hardly feel anything. There was so much happening every day, so much to take in relentlessly, all the time, he couldn't even picture what his parents might be doing. As though they were someone else's parents, not the two people he longed for most.

What do you think? Aditya laughed.

There had been an email the other day: *How are you, call.*

He walked out of office hours in tears. He'd met with the machine learning professor, he'd taken care to write questions in full sentences and embarrassingly read them from his notepad—How does logistic regression work?—and the professor, instead of answering his questions, had asked him about weights, intending to derive an explanation from his answer. He'd studied limits, he knew the answer to the professor's question, the words forming in his mouth were beginning coherently enough and he was surprised by that, but then there weren't any more phrases, just long pauses, fillers, sweat dripping down his shirt, his mind utterly blank, the professor staring at him, waiting for him to answer this fundamental question. That's when he saw it, the thing that crossed the professor's face, the thing that broke him: pity. The professor told him to go through a basic calculus text, to catch up before the upcoming midterm because it carried 40 percent of the grade and it would only get much harder from here, and he'd left, nodding sheepishly, unable to look up from his feet.

He came to a stop on the sidewalk and inspected a fallen red leaf, crisp at the edges, the size of his palm, as real as the drops

in his eyes. How could there be so many colors? He picked it up.
An ant scurried out from the curved edge, and he gently put the
leaf back on the ground.

The temperature dropped to the fifties, and he took to wearing
his one sweater everywhere. Nice fucking weather, Nargie said,
taking off his own jacket.

The rumor came quick after that. Nobody knew where it
came from, but everybody heard it—the restaurant would fold
soon. There will be something else, Jose said. Nargie shrugged.
We always find something else, Pedro said, more in response to
Aditya's face than what he felt. It'll be fine, Aditya said, echo-
ing them. They worked in silence. The slide of tomatoes, the
hem of garlic, the skin of a chicken, water running over nails,
oil-greased fingers, a good day's work touched him, quiet and
alone. Exiting the restaurant, he saw a man walking in the other
direction with a back that looked exactly like his father's. Short
neck, wide shoulders, dark skin. It wasn't him, impossible, he
knew that, but his heart sped all the same. He followed the man
into unfamiliar streets, exhilarated. After ten minutes of walking, he stopped. The man receded from his eyes, and he exhaled
into the quiet dark. Where am I, Father?

To his left, a mobile store. He couldn't help himself; he pur-
chased a calling card, stealing ten dollars from rent and utili-
ties and the occasional grocery. He called his father right away,
fingers pressing the wrong access code, backtracking, pressing
the right numbers, the phone ringing lifting helloing, the hello
of his father warming his ear, his father's voice breaking with
excitement, shouting for his mother.

A car passed by and he glanced at it, and something came over him swiftly, a mysterious darkness wrung his chest, he couldn't speak, he couldn't tell them how his life was, he couldn't answer their questions about whether he was okay and if he missed them, he found his attention drifting, he wasn't hearing what his father was saying, an ocean suddenly engulfed him, his eyes began to water, then a bus went by, and he chanced upon a small raft floating in the ocean, he held on to it tightly and said he had to go, he was very busy, everything was fine, school was great, he'd call later. He hung up.

Silence, hunger. He'd foregone his share of leftovers at the restaurant and returned to the apartment early so he could study for his midterm the next day. He flipped through his notebook and copied the alien symbols, but they remained just as alien. He'd been unable to help Mani with an assignment they were partners on earlier that week, and in the computer lab the night before, sitting alone in the last row, he'd overheard Mani telling somebody that he'd had to do the whole assignment himself, the superlong one, because his roommate didn't know shit.

He looked through his class notes and tried to make sense of it. Useless. He might as well go to the park and watch the sunset. It was cold, but every time he looked at Mani's mattress in the room, he remembered how he'd sat behind the computer, frozen, waiting for the night to be over, typing and erasing *didn't know shit* until he could leave undetected. And so he left for the park. Maybe Toby the dog could become more like the robotic dog equipped with AI and bark all the shits he needed to know in his face.

By the time he got to the park, the evening light was dying, and Toby was nowhere in sight. He searched for the mother desperately as if she were his mother and he, her infant. A mild pain in his chest, and he crumbled onto the grass, the bench farther away than he could manage. Inside his head—everything pushed inside his head in this fucking country—there were two options. He could return home to India a failure and watch his mother die. Or he could stay and watch himself die, slowly, dispassionately. That was the choice.

The sky faded orange, moths flew around his leg, and the wind made him sneeze. He watched the moths leave, one after the other. The lamp near the bench had turned on; that was perhaps where the moths had gone. It glowed, just like a light-house, which reminded him of a journey he'd once taken, not the journey he'd taken to come to this country, but a different one maybe, he couldn't really tell, all journeys had come to resemble one another, the thing uniting them being the distance, all of it farther and farther from where he sat now, the only thing left of the evening this light in front of him, the one that shed and shed to reach his eyes.

He rose and brushed the dirt off his knees, ready to do what-ever it took. To walk until he was home.

Summers of Waiting

I

It was summer again. Dust flew to greet Sita's eyes as she stepped off the flight. In the taxi that would take her home to the village, heat shot through the car window, singeing her skin. She held her forearms against the sun. The last time Sita had been in India, her grandfather had been eighty-two. "I am ready," Thatha had said in a moment of clarity, the blood pressure monitor she brought from the States listening to the dictates of his heart. This time, a year later, she hoped she'd reach home before it was too late: not the village, not the house, but *Thatha*.

When she was in the States, they never spoke. He said he couldn't hear her over the phone. The only time they'd spoken on the phone had been when she'd first arrived as a college freshman. Thrice, she'd told him that she'd landed in Chicago. In return, she'd heard a barrage of hellos, a silence, and a beep of disconnection. From then on, it was Manga, the maid, who answered, who told her how he was. It wasn't much different when Sita came home either; he barely spoke. Not for any one particular reason. It was the sort of distance that opened up between people who loved each other so much that they had to let each other go.

Except Sita didn't let go. Her parents had died when she was a child, and Thatha was all she had. Twelve years had passed since she'd first left home for a boarding school in Hyderabad, six of those years in the States, and she'd come back to the village every one of those twelve summers, but all that heat had done nothing: Thatha stayed cold.

The taxi honked past other vehicles exiting the terminal. Sita felt her stomach churn. This was maybe her last opportunity to speak with Thatha. Manga had told her how much Thatha had deteriorated in the past year. He was even less coherent than before; his hands shook so much that he couldn't be trusted to hold a glass of water. He'd need somebody to watch him in the evenings after Manga cooked and left. Sita wished she could stay with him until the end, but she couldn't afford it—she had debts to pay, high-interest college loans. She appreciated a lot about the States, had even managed to make a couple of friends, but being there felt like exile. Even in the smallest of things, she felt it. When she was growing up, she'd barely noticed the detergent bar they used in the village, a local brand smelling of soapy citrus, but in the States, she'd come to miss the smell—the fruity artificiality of it. She'd tried to order it online but couldn't find it. There were days when she would arrive at her apartment, tired from working, and relax by searching for soap on the internet. The other bars, she quickly found, weren't artificial enough. Part of her knew that she would never find the soap in the States, that she would find it only in the village, but she continued to look to the point where the only ads she got in her browser were for detergent.

The taxi bustled through the traffic, moving past city buses and motorcycles and auto-rickshaws. Sita's eyes fell on the billboards on top of the buildings. Advertisements for fairness creams, motorcycles, action movies. She'd had enough of ads—she worked in advertising operations for a media company in Chicago. It wasn't the best job; she had only two weeks of vacation per year, and the journey here took two days of that. Twelve days was all she had. Twelve days to be with Thatha. She leaned her head against the window.

II

The year was 1965. Or perhaps 1964. Thatha couldn't immediately tell where his memories had led him. When he touched the wicker chair on the veranda or the dining table, or sometimes when he held an object with his hands, be it a key chain or a wooden cane, he found himself in the middle of clouds. Soft to the touch, they surrounded him with a thin mist that lay on his hands like early-morning dew. After a while the mist would lift and he'd see the past again. Days he had long forgotten and years he wished to forget. A film ran over his eyes. Blurry snapshots, vivid feelings, ringing voices. He had no choice in what came through the haze. Something always did, and he was grateful it took him away.

A brick wall emerged. Engraved into the wall, an inscription plate that said SATYA NILAYA, "the house where Satya lives," Satya being Sita's father. Hibiscus flowers strung in a garland around the inscription wilted in the air. Petals lay strewn everywhere. The garland swung like a ghost. The gate stood open, and stray cattle fed on the grass in the yard. A young Thatha shuffled in with a framed photo of his wife in his left arm and the baby Satya in his right arm leaning against his chest. Behind him came a brother and a couple of cousins.

One of the cousins shooed the cattle away and closed the

gate. "Come back to my hut, at least for a few more months," the brother said.

Thatha stepped inside the house with the baby. The doorway was too low for his six-and-a-half-foot frame; he had to bend to get through. He'd sped through the construction process when he learned he was to become a father. His wife wanted Satya's first footsteps to be in a proper house, not the kind of thatched hut they lived in—he lived in. She'd had so many desires in life— why endometriosis, why her?

The first cousin touched him on the shoulder. "Let me take the baby."

Thatha shook his head. "Get me a nail and a hammer."

"It's not auspicious to start living in a new house," the second cousin said. "It hasn't even been a month since her body turned to ash—"

"Where is the hammer?"

The brother said, "Enough, let's go back."

"You go back. I'll stay here with my son." Thatha hunted for a hammer, Satya sleeping on his right arm. He couldn't add extra work to his brother's wife or anyone else for that matter. This was what his parents had constantly fought over, his mother tired from taking care of his cousins as if they were her children too.

"The boy will need the care of a woman," the first cousin said.

"We are not asking you to marry again right away, but after a couple of months. Don't be so stubborn, live with one of us until then," the second cousin said.

"There it is." Thatha located the hammer on the shelf. He set down the framed photo and picked up the hammer with his left arm. He stopped. It wouldn't be possible to hit a nail with it while also holding Satya.

The brother stepped forward and extended his arms, asking for the baby. "You cannot raise him all by yourself."

The brother moved for the baby, and Thatha stepped back. He wouldn't give him up. He put the hammer down and picked up a nail with his free hand. He walked a few feet to the living room wall, keeping his gaze on his brother, and held the nail at the edge of his fist and stabbed the wall repeatedly. He pushed the nail in with his hard fist, and the nail found enough of a hold to keep from falling down. Thatha picked up the hammer with his left hand and tapped at the nail, all the while looking at his brother. "I don't need another woman."

Thatha grabbed the framed photo and hung it on the nail. He pointed at the photo. "That is my wife, and this is my home. Now, get out."

As he was leaving, the brother stopped at the doorway. "The frame is a little tilted," he said, then left with the cousins.

Thatha watched them go past the gate. He returned to the living room and set about aligning the photo. He couldn't look at her as he did so. The black-and-white photo, a close-up taken at an exhibition that passed through their village, was of poor quality. You could barely see the scar on her cheek. But he didn't need the photo; he knew every pore on her nose, each curve in her ear. He was afraid of time, though, and what it might do to his memory of her. What it had already done to him. His love of ten years now gone, except in a photo that put a knife through his chest every time he looked at it. A sob quivered through his body. Satya stirred, and Thatha put his left hand behind the baby's neck. Satya opened his eyes, and there she was. Thatha lifted Satya a little higher and looked at him—the photo behind the baby, on the wall, now relegated to an outline. He had the boy.

Until he didn't.

Now Thatha was back on the veranda of the house, old and alone. The clouds entirely gone. No mist on his hands. The sun shone brightly near his feet.

He tried to hold on to the image of Satya as a baby, but it slipped into the light.

III

On the highway, dust came through the windows. The driver asked Sita if it was true that there was no dust in the States. She laughed and said not like here.

The driver, encouraged by her laugh, asked her what life was like in the States. Did everybody have a car? His questions reminded her of the ones she faced in Chicago. People at work, or even her friends, if they met up at an Indian restaurant, for instance, would look at her and wonder what a certain dish was made of or ask her why Bollywood movies had so many songs. She was no expert. When she tried to answer, she realized she wasn't able to convey what she innately understood. Playing the role of an Indian ambassador made her feel like an imposter. It was the same the few times she went on a date: I grew up in a small village and moved here blah blah, India has many different languages blah blah. She was forever explaining something that would remain unexplainable. She didn't know what it was, but she felt it. Like the time she had a minor retinal surgery and was blinded for a day, she could sense that light was flooding the room from somewhere, but didn't know, couldn't tell, where it came from.

Sita said to the driver that some people had cars, not

everybody, and looked out the window. Rice fields and tele-phone poles. She watched them go past, field after field, pole after pole, until her eyes drifted over the horizon.

She imagined their house in the village. The mahogany porch, the yard, the cement walls, and Thatha in his wicker chair sitting on the veranda. Memories took her home before her body got there. Her brain did this every time she came back.

She traced the space between her and Thatha. Part of the distance—there were two parts to this, Sita didn't like to think about the other part—was the weight of things that had hap-pened, the death of her parents and what that had done to Tha-tha. There was nothing she could do about that part, maybe there was nothing she could do about the whole thing. All she could do was remember him, what he had been to her.

There was the story he told her when she was an eight-year-old and couldn't sleep. A story about giants and tree fairies.

His hands would widen as he began, and his eyes would come alive. "Once upon a time, in the Vindhya mountains, there was a kingdom of giants, the shortest of them still at least ten feet tall . . ."

His opening line never changed. The story was, depending on the moment, an entertainment, a childhood fable, an embar-rassment, a shared past, a way to understand her grandfather, and the closest she could ever get to him. Sita hadn't understood why Thatha was so drawn to that story until much later. In the story, a giant father looks for his lost son until he is cursed to be a tree, searching for him in every object he touches.

She'd ask Thatha, "Did you tell this story to Dad too? When he was a kid?"

Thatha would nod.

"What did he say? Did he cry at the end too?"

The light in Thatha's eyes would dim, and she'd learned not to ask him about her father.

Thatha often hadn't responded when, as a teenager, she'd asked if she could attend the local school instead of the boarding school she'd been sent to. But he'd always responded when she'd ask for the story. And with every telling, he'd inject some new bit of backstory, a slight variation, a newer segment that filled the air around them like a tall, imperious giant whose existence demanded belief.

Six and a half feet tall at his straightest, and two and a half feet wide at his widest, Thatha himself was something of a giant. Summer mornings as a child, when Sita overslept, on a double-folded woolen blanket out on the terrace, oblivious to the chatter of birds and families, Thatha would lean over her, waiting for her to wake. She'd open her eyes to find him looming near her, his face bigger than the yellow ball of sun behind it, and he himself an umbrella against the burning rays. In the afternoons, when Thatha would take a nap, she'd run her toy car over his sprawling bare back, which was infinitely smoother than the surrounding ground. She'd pretend to fall, but his hand would be ready to protect her, a safety railing. And at night they'd sit beneath a light bulb on the front porch, preparing pulihora. She'd stretch out her hand, and Thatha, vigorously mixing tamarind paste, rice, and salt on a steel plate, would pause and give her a morsel, the nail of his index finger holding within it the light bulb's reflection.

Later, when she'd returned from boarding school for summer holidays, days were duller. There wasn't enough of Thatha in them, even though he sat right in the living room staring at the portraits on the wall. And when she was away from home, at the boarding school for the rest of the year, Thatha was like the moon, his presence all over the sky, his absence shining inside her.

IV

It was the mid-nineties, 1994 or 1995 or 1996, Thatha couldn't say. Clouds curved under his palm. He saw a newspaper through the haze.

The state government had put out a notice in the newspaper. Satya had become a teacher by then, and all the teachers in the district had been ordered to read a bunch of material and take a test to better their pay grade. Satya began studying late into the night, long after Ramani, Sita's mother, slept. Thatha pretended to have trouble sleeping in those days, stayed up reading the Gita just to give Satya company. But every so often he'd fall asleep, the book sliding down his dhoti and waking him up.

In the afternoon, little Sita wouldn't let her exhausted father take a nap. Satya's eyes were red like the earth.

Thatha took Sita outside. "Don't disturb your father, he needs to sleep. What do you want?"

"I-skeem," she said.

"It's not good for your throat," he said, but he knew she wouldn't listen, just like Satya, the only difference being that back in the day there was no ice cream, and Satya had wanted peechu mithai instead; he'd cry until Thatha bought him a stick. How similar they were.

She whined. He walked her to a store and bought a vanilla cup, but wouldn't give it to her. "Promise me," he said.

"Pomise." Sita reached for the ice cream.

"No, promise—with an 'r.'"

"Pomise."

Thatha held back the ice cream, and Sita began to cry. Thatha held out his hand. "Okay, promise me. Not a word to your mother. She doesn't need to know."

Sita smiled and put her hand in his. "Pomise."

He watched her eat the ice cream as slowly as possible. He made a mental note to buy groceries; Ramani had reminded him the other day that they were running out of dal. He'd take Sita with him to the store in the evening. She'd enjoy that. He used to take Satya everywhere with him, to the paddy fields, to the classroom, to the bank, to the point where if he went somewhere alone, he felt like he was missing an arm. She reminded him of those days.

Sita finished the ice cream, and they went home.

Ramani asked Sita as soon as she ran inside, "Did you have ice cream?"

Sita shook her head.

Ramani turned to Thatha at the doorstep. "You bought her ice cream again?"

Thatha took off his sandals. "She said that?"

"I'm her mother. I can tell when she's lying."

Thatha entered the house and sat in a chair.

"You're spoiling her," Ramani said.

Satya came out of the bedroom. Ramani looked at Satya and said, "You tell your father, he doesn't understand parenting."

Thatha glared at Ramani. "I know how to raise a child."

They all fell silent. Sita opened her hand and blew at it: "Pomise gone."

Satya laughed. Thatha began laughing with him, and Ramani contained her smile. Thatha caught Sita's hand and tickled her.

He could make out, even as Sita squealed with joy, a note of contentment in Satya's laughter.

Back in the present, Thatha took in the dining table. "Satya," he said, still hearing him laugh. There was a plate of partially eaten curry in front of him, flies hovering over it.

He finished the last morsel and stepped away from the table.

V

The taxi swerved past a bullock cart carrying sugarcane, and the bridge that marked the beginning of her village came into view. Sita felt the tingly anticipation of arrival. Chickens ran wild as the taxi approached the courtyard. Manga, bent over a marble slate where she was washing clothes, abandoned the laundry and rushed to greet her. Manga's kid, seven-year-old Suresh, was sitting on a rock next to the slate. Sita always brought him chocolates.

"You've become so thin!" Manga said, clutching her hand.

"No, I'm the same," Sita said with a smile. Even as Sita insisted that she could get the suitcase herself, Manga grabbed it.

Thatha stepped outside, leaning on the wooden cane Sita had given him on her last visit. He looked worse than he had the previous summer. His back appeared more bent, his face further darkened. He didn't have his glasses on; he must have been sleeping. He held his hand to his eyebrows to shut out the sun and looked at her. A smile grew on his face and he walked forward. Sita smiled back; this was better than last time.

As Thatha drew closer, his face mellowed and he stopped walking. She understood that seeing her, as always, reminded him of his dead son.

"How was your journey?" Thatha asked. He was looking her way, but his eyes were unfocused.

"Good," Sita said.

"How long until you have to go back to college?" he asked.

Sita looked at him. He no longer had a perception of time; he'd forgotten that she'd already graduated. She didn't think there was any point in correcting him. "Two weeks."

He nodded. He sat on a wicker chair on the veranda and looked at the street.

Sita walked inside. Everything seemed well kept, except for the clock on the mantelpiece. It showed 7:20 when it was almost noon. She was in the village of stopped clocks. It had been the same way the last time she was here. At her relatives' house down the street, the clock had been stuck at 8:34. They'd served her tea and asked how far Dallas was from where she lived and showed her pictures of their children and grandchildren, all of whom lived in the States. Almost every house on the street held a family with children or grandchildren in the States. The houses were plush with all the luxuries the immigrants would need when they returned for vacation: AC units and Wi-Fi, things the old people had no need of. When the sons arrived, AC units turned themselves on and the clocks fixed themselves. After they left, the AC units switched off and the clocks drew to a halt. Like the old people left behind, the clocks suspended their lives and lay in wait until they were brought back to life.

Sita went to her bedroom: a large, sparse room with a double cot bed, an almirah, and French windows. She opened the almirah to see her mother's Kanchi sarees. Sita had already taken some of them with her to the States—not to wear, but to keep them next to her, to feel the worn silk in her hands. The black salwar kameez she'd forgotten to pack lay on a shelf in the almirah, neatly folded.

She heard Thatha's walking stick tap the floor. After each tap, a long pause. Thatha stopped in the hallway, bent to avoid hitting his head, and gingerly walked through the crimson ribbed archway.

Sita asked Thatha, "Why didn't we ever get a taller doorway built?"

As if noticing it for the first time, Thatha stopped to look at the archway. He touched the doorframe with his right hand and limped into the hall, letting his hand graze through. He seemed not to register Sita's presence. It was as if he were already gone.

She sat on the floor and pulled at her suitcase. She unpacked her clothes. By the time she put the suitcase away, the temple gongs rang. It was a sound Sita hadn't known she'd miss. She knew, from previous summers, that the sights and sounds of home would be more pronounced the first day. The human brain had a habit of normalizing everything. Time would speed up the next day. Days would devolve into breakfasts, lunches, and dinners. Nights would vanish in sleep. Her twelve days would disintegrate into moments of active consciousness that flickered here and there. But Sita couldn't keep her eyes open. She went to bed, unable to fight jet lag.

VI

August 27, 1997. Thatha knew right away where the haze took him. He'd been there enough times. None of it hurt anymore; he felt nothing. He lay on the bed and stared at the ceiling fan, let the film wash over him.

Sprained ankle. The day after Sita turned six, Thatha slipped in the bathroom. He sprained his ankle and couldn't walk. The doctor came and wrapped a bandage around his foot. Thatha had been planning to go to a wedding later that day, the wedding of his friend's son. He had promised to be there, and so he asked Satya and Ramani to attend the wedding on his behalf. They refused to go. When he insisted, saying it would be inappropriate for no one from the family to attend, Satya reluctantly had agreed.

Sita didn't lift her eyes when her parents bid her goodbye; she was playing with a doll she'd placed on Thatha's resting back. Soon after they left, she fell asleep on him. Thatha couldn't move without waking her up, and so he lay still as the pond in front of their house. After she awoke, Thatha turned around and opened the bandage a little. He sat up and tried to put pressure on his leg and winced in pain.

The school headmaster, Satya's colleague, knocked on the open door. Sita ran to him and then came back. The headmaster looked ill.

"Did you hurt yourself too?" Thatha smiled.

The headmaster scratched his temple, and Thatha gestured toward his bandage. Sita took her toy car and played with it.

"There's bad news," the headmaster said.

"What is it?"

"The bus Satya went in." The headmaster paused.

Thatha stared at him.

The headmaster said, "It fell into a gorge."

Thatha didn't move.

"My nephew, the police inspector, just called." The headmaster sat next to Thatha.

"No, no. It's probably a different bus," Thatha said.

"He saw them."

Sita drove the car in circles. Thatha took a step toward the door and collapsed on the ground. His bandage came apart and his mouth opened in a loud cry.

Now, many years later, the dampness on his hands had disappeared, but his mouth stayed open. He rose from the bed and reached for a glass of water.

VII

The heat was incessant, the air at once blazing and numbing. The days were simultaneously long and short, empty and momentous. Sita had inspected the entire house. She had dusted everything and washed the bedsheets in Thatha's room. She gave Manga some money and told her to take a few days off. She looked at Thatha's medicines and filled his pill box. She spoke with the neighbors next door and paid them to check in on Thatha in the evenings after she went back to the States. She cooked and cleaned. There was nothing else to do, nobody else to talk to.

Thatha slept most of the day. He'd have breakfast and fall asleep sitting in a chair in the living room. In the afternoon, he coughed for a while and took a nap in his room. Evenings, he sat on the veranda for a couple of hours, and she couldn't tell if his eyes took in anything. When she sat next to him and tried talking, his head didn't turn. It was as if she were invisible.

There wasn't much for Sita to do except sift through the memories contained within the house. In the living room, she found her old notebooks, full of drawings and math problems in her cursive handwriting. She opened one and saw that she'd written her entire address under her name on the first page:

Sita Kuchipudi,
House no: 1-8-750/3/2, Cheruvu Road,
Nagayalanka,
Krishna District,
Andhra Pradesh,
India,
Earth,
Milky Way,
Universe

She laughed louder than she normally would and looked at Thatha in the living room chair to see if he'd heard her. He had not. His eyes were closed, and his head moved every few seconds, a tiny bit to the left or the right.

She reached for the next notebook and found behind it a toy car, the one she'd played with as a child.

She'd played with it the day her parents died. She'd cried a lot. She remembered thinking if she hadn't cried all the time for ice cream, God wouldn't have punished her by taking her parents away. The headmaster held a bawling Thatha that day. Someone came and took her inside. She couldn't see anything; tears clouded her vision. Thatha's brother and his family came over. There was a lot happening; she didn't understand any of it. People kept arriving and they were all crying too. Her parents had been found in a ravine with some of the bus's wreckage, and the police carried Thatha to the morgue to identify their bodies. She tried to go too, but she wasn't allowed. Someone handed her a glass of milk and asked her to drink. She refused and stood by the front door crying, waiting for Thatha to return. At some point, she fell asleep, and someone picked her up and put her in a bed.

When Thatha returned, strangers carried him. He didn't talk to anyone; his eyes were soggy, and his mouth was open. He kept repeating, as if in a trance, "I killed them." When she went up to him and shook his arm, his eyes were vacant. "I killed them," he said. Thatha didn't speak much after that day.

Sita looked up and saw him dozing still in the chair.

She flipped through another notebook.

She stopped at a drawing she'd done of her and Thatha. They were stick figures, one small one lying on the chest of a tall one. The day she'd drawn it, it had rained so much that water leaked through the roof of her classroom. The school had closed, and parents came with umbrellas and picked up their children. She'd waited for someone to come, all alone in the school building. She was only six. It had been about two weeks since her parents had died, and Thatha wasn't himself, lost in his head all the time, and everybody else had been picked up. She cried. She'd walked herself to school and back every day for those two weeks, and there was food the relatives had brought, and she'd managed fine. And she'd have walked in the rain too, but there was thunder and she was afraid of thunder.

It was also getting dark, cloudy dark, and she decided it was better to walk in the rain than wait in the dark. She'd taken a few steps in the rain when she saw Thatha running to her, barefoot with an umbrella over his head. He whisked her home and rubbed her wet hair with a towel and let her sleep on his chest. He patted her on the shoulder when a sob escaped her. And then she was fine. But she hadn't wanted to tell him that she was fine; she was afraid that would release him and he would disappear again into his grief. She lay listening to the steady hum of rain on the roof, the rip of thunder obliterating every other sound. She wasn't scared of the thunder anymore, but she didn't want to hear it either. She listened, her ear burrowed in Thatha's chest hair, to the staccato beat of his heart gently rocking her to sleep.

Sita went through the rest of the notebooks, some from her boarding school years. In each one, below her name, she'd written her exact age, to the day. Thatha had done that; when the boarding school admissions officer had asked how old she was, he'd briefly counted on his fingers and announced that she was one month and three days short of twelve years. Thatha survived on these things. Numbers and facts were like potatoes that could be held in one's hand and examined. Loss and grief weren't like that. And she, in his unstated opinion, was better off studying the former. Her boarding school notebooks were filled with long equations and random scribbles. Her whole life had been studying then, except when she'd come home in the summer, and Thatha was doing his retirement thing (he'd sold off their land and put the money in a bank and steadily drew from it), and they spent their afternoons each in their own world, not speaking much, him staring into space, and her doodling all over a notebook, and it was already evident that the whole summer was going to be exactly that, reflection after reflection, and in fact all summers from then on would be nothing but a jumping-off point for them—each summer infused with echoes of summers past, each looking for another time they had once lived.

VIII

The sun set for the day, after threatening to burn them all down. Sita sat in the wicker chair on the veranda with a novel. The novel was about reincarnation, and she found herself enjoying it more than she'd expected. Soon, it was dark. She stopped reading. Fireflies glowed around the edges of grass in the corner of the courtyard. Bicycles tinkled in the distance. Voices reached Sita from inside. Thatha had turned on the news. He did that every once in a while. She didn't know how much of it he registered. But soon a buzzing went through the electric wires and darkness enveloped the village. She could hear the croaking of frogs, as if the power cut had turned off the lights but turned on the sound.

Thatha stepped out and sat in the wicker chair next to Sita. She saw his face in the dark—a blank, as always.

"How frequently do these power cuts happen?" she asked him.

"Tuesday, Wednesday, and Sunday nights," he answered.

Sita grew excited. A coherent Thatha. Questions were the only way she could get him to talk. Some people broadcast their stories, demanding to be heard. Thatha was not like that; he was a reluctant storyteller. Even when she was a little girl, he'd tell a story only when Sita asked. It was as if he could access it only when someone located it within him. Like a computer, he needed someone to click the file open.

"Thatha, do you remember the story you used to tell me?" Sita asked.

Thatha blinked.

"The story of the giant. Could you tell it to me again now?"

But Thatha was staring into space again; he'd drifted out of himself, gone somewhere she couldn't reach.

IX

The heat wave intensified. It was the summer of death. Ants carried off dead cockroaches. Birds stayed put in trees, refusing to fly, except for a crow, which dropped dead on the street. Stray dogs heaved under the shade of trees, refusing to get up and inspect the dead crow. Two cows died, collapsing on the way back from whatever remained of the pond. The news channels reported hundreds of deaths. Two streets away, an elderly lady had died in the middle of the night and been discovered by her maid the next morning. The hot air carried death with it, singing a lullaby at everything interested.

The heat crept into people and stayed long after the day had ended. Sita could feel it in her, a low boil. Thatha coughed long and hard. She'd taken him to the hospital the last time she'd come home. The doctors ran a bunch of tests and concluded that there wasn't anything particularly wrong with him; he was simply old. Thatha coughed again in a long burst, and Sita went to his room. "Do you need anything? Cough syrup?" she asked.

He was lying on the bed without a shirt and looked up at her, then down at the bedside table. She grabbed the cough syrup on the table and poured some into a glass. She sat on the bed and put her hand behind his warm neck, brought the glass to his mouth with the other. She observed him, her giant of a Thatha, taking little sips like a helpless infant. She laid his head back on the pillow and watched as his coughing eased. She sat next to him for a long time as he slept, breathing in and out. She held his arm and remembered holding his hand as a child.

In those days, Sita had always accompanied Thatha on trips to the local store. They bought bread, milk, and other groceries. She made him buy chocolates occasionally. If the bill ran to nineteen rupees and fifty paise, Thatha would take out two ten-rupee notes from his shirt pocket and give her the money, because she insisted on handling all transactions. She'd count the money carefully and put it on a toffee box on the shelf. The shopkeeper would take it and return two twenty-five-paise coins. She'd think furiously and select two toffees, twenty-five paise each. She would eat one on the way back and keep the other for another day. Sometimes, when the bill didn't produce change, she'd ask Thatha if he had any. She'd withdraw her hand from his and open her palm. Thatha would grope in his pocket, and then she'd count as his fingers placed one coin at a time in her outstretched hand.

When she was a child, Thatha had been her property—until she'd turned eleven and everything between them had changed. When he'd said he no longer had "the strength" to take care of her and sent her to boarding school the following year.

What actually happened was something Sita didn't like to think about.

She'd gotten her period when she was eleven. She'd been painting a dead grasshopper on the veranda and become aware of a growing discomfort. But she'd been so caught up in getting the legs right that she ignored the cramp until she could no longer tolerate it. She got up and saw a drop of blood dripping down her legs, onto the floor. It came from her underwear, and she felt certain that she was dying. She ran shouting for Thatha.

Thatha got up from his bed and saw the red spot on the floor where Sita had been sitting.

"I'm dying," Sita said, and began to cry.

Thatha's face became thin. He put on a shirt over his baniyan and said, "Stay here."

Sita walked behind him to the door.

Thatha said, "Don't step out of the house."

She saw him walking down the street, to his cousin's house— his brother had died of a heart attack the year before. Five minutes later, a couple of ladies, their relatives, came. There was no sign of Thatha. The ladies took her inside and told her what it meant, that it was okay. They mopped the floor where the blood had fallen and stayed with her. Thatha returned later that night. By then, she was already asleep, confused and distraught.

The next morning, she woke up and saw that the ladies had left. She saw Thatha resting on his stomach, and she ran to him. She sat on his back and hit him on the shoulder for leaving her with people she didn't trust.

"Get up, get up," Thatha said.

"Where did you go?" Sita pinched him in the back.

"Do you not understand? Get up, it's not appropriate," Thatha said, pushing her away.

Sita stepped away in tears. This was not the Thatha she knew. Later that evening, when she went to him on the veranda and held his hand, Thatha wouldn't close his hand around hers. He didn't say anything, but she felt a reluctance within him. She felt she was being punished.

The next day, when Thatha slept, Sita stared at him. She considered apologizing for the blood, for making a mess throughout the house, for making him go in shame. But she had a feeling he wouldn't listen, he wouldn't understand. Why did he do this to her? She became angry. Right below Thatha's shirt hung up on a nail, she saw a ten-rupee note lying on the floor. She tiptoed past him and grabbed it. She walked to the store and returned with a bag full of toffees.

Thatha stood on the veranda when she walked in. Her heart dropped—she'd thought he would still be asleep.

"What's in the bag?" he asked.

She showed him.

"Where did you get those toffees?"

"I bought them."

Thatha slapped her wrist. "Did you take the ten-rupee note from my shirt?"

She began crying. "No."

"Stop crying and tell me the truth. You stole!"

Thatha had never shouted at her before. And Sita grew angry again; he was the one who had betrayed her trust. "I didn't steal," she said.

"You stole money from my shirt!"

"I didn't," she said.

"You're a liar." Thatha hit her on the wrist.

Sita was furious that he'd hit her after abandoning her. After pushing her away, after not touching her. She wanted to hurt him. She didn't know what she was saying, until after she had said it. "You killed my parents!"

Thatha froze. He took a step back and crumpled into a chair. "I killed them."

"I'm sorry." Sita pulled at Thatha's knees.

It didn't matter that she apologized several times. It didn't matter that she cried at his feet, begging him to forgive her. It didn't matter that she offered him water to drink, her tears slipping into the tumbler. Nothing worked. Thatha's face went still, his eyes became impenetrable. There would no longer be coins dropping into Sita's outstretched palm. There would no longer be anything for her to hold.

X

Sometime in 2003. Thatha knew the year, but not the month or the date. That was the year he'd sent Sita away to a boarding school where she'd get better care and education. Mist lined his fingers. Through the haze, he saw his brother and Sita talking.

His little Sita doodling in a notebook at the same time. Satya's cheeks and nose.

"When are you going to boarding school?" Thatha's brother asked Sita.

"Never." Sita grew sullen.

"Day after tomorrow," Thatha said.

"Why not let her be here? She doesn't like the idea at all."

"She needs discipline. I'm too old."

Sita began to protest. "No—"

"Go inside now." Thatha cut her off.

When Sita reluctantly went inside the house, Thatha's brother said to Thatha, "Can you live without her?"

Thatha stayed silent. He knew it would be difficult. But there was no way around it. He could not get on with life pretending she was a version of his son. Sita was no longer a child, she was becoming a woman, and they were living in a society; he couldn't behave with her the way he did with Satya. He could not hit her and later caress her as he had with Satya, he could not take her everywhere, he couldn't hold her hand whenever he wanted. "It's necessary. Someday she'll marry and go away anyway."

Thatha's brother nodded.

"My energy is over," Thatha said, looking at the sky. All his life, he had told stories: first to Satya, and then to Sita. Stories in which the giant keeps looking—first for his wife, and then for his son. Both of whom were dead, long gone. He was tired of telling stories, tired of being left behind, tired of holding on to life with all his might. The dam he built against grief burst through and the years struck him afresh.

XI

Sita had four more days at home before she had to return to the States. This knowledge made her queasy. She had to find a way with Thatha. She watched from the sidewall as a stream of ladies in colorful sarees, with jasmine flowers in their hair, walked to the temple. She vaguely remembered going to the temple with her mother as a child. It was early in the morning, but the sun was strong. Sita felt dizzy and went inside to lie down. She closed her eyes and fell asleep.

She dreamed she was in a container ship. The ship was going somewhere, she didn't know where. She was chained. The chains originated from a fitted latch inside, and there was a lot of hay next to her. She looked around the edges of the hay as if expecting a chicken to pop out and wander around. The container was white inside, but the paint came off near the chain to reveal a metallic gray. There weren't any windows. If there were, she could have tried to stand up and see outside. There was nothing else in the container. Just her and the hay. The container was blue on the outside. She somehow knew that, even though she couldn't see it. She also knew she was on a ship full of containers. It was as if she could see outside and inside at once. She saw Thatha walking outside with his cane. She cried for him to open the locked container and let her out. He stopped, wiped his nose, and continued walking. She screamed with all the power in her lungs. She heard the sound of laughter from outside. It wasn't mocking her; it was the laughter of people far away. It flooded the container and pushed her eyes open.

She rose from the bed. It was Thatha, laughing. And Manga's kid, Suresh, laughing with him. Sita stepped out to where she could see the two of them. Her eyes fell on Thatha's fingers, which gripped the boy's arm, just as he'd held hers when she was a girl. Thatha had a cricket ball in one hand; he brought it to his eyes to examine it, then handed it to the boy, who took it and ran.

Sita's anger rose like the sun. She stormed over to Thatha. "Why did you give up on me?"

He looked at her and smiled. His hearing had gotten worse. "What are you saying?"

A breeze blew through, and his eyes dipped. He was lost again.

"Why did you distance yourself from me?" Sita asked, but she knew as she was saying it that there would not be an answer. A hot breeze swept through the veranda, swaying the bell of a cud-chewing buffalo that was passing by. The buffalo stopped in front of the courtyard and looked at Sita and Thatha with sad eyes. Perhaps it was reflecting her own grief. A cowherd in a dhoti ushered it forward.

Thatha pointed at the buffalo. "Satya," he said.

The heat had dazed her, and the absurdity of Thatha's actions didn't register until she turned to look at him. He stared straight ahead. The heat instantly swallowed a teardrop that had rolled from his eye. She felt her anger rising again, although she knew that Thatha had mixed up the fable he used to tell her with his very real grief. He saw his son everywhere: in the living room wall, on the dining table surface, in the wooden cane she gave him, on a fallen neem leaf drifting in the wind, and, now, in a buffalo. Thatha, living the story, could not see the one thing in which his son still lived: her.

Sita stomped inside, past the portraits she could never look at. She went to her room, which was cooler than it was outside, but she continued to feel the heat in her stomach. In her skin.

In her eyes. She felt it simmering to a rage. Rage against the dying and rage against the dead. She felt like screaming, *Begone, stories! Begone, dead!*

Her mother would have understood. She wouldn't have hidden behind a story, as Thatha did. She'd had a nice, short life. She didn't lack for anything. She wasn't the storytelling type, though she did leave a story behind, and Sita was the one who carried it.

XII

Night fell, with no trace of the moon. It was as if the heat had tricked the moon into thinking the sun was still out. Sita stood in the kitchen, cutting vegetables for dinner. Thatha wandered in from his room, his hand reaching for a glass.

"Thatha, I'd have gotten water for you," Sita said.

She took the glass, had barely filled it, when Thatha collapsed to the floor like he'd been shot.

Sita rushed to him. His eyes were half-open, and he coughed and breathed through his mouth. Sita ran to the phone and called for the car. After she called, she heard him gasp for air. The driver, their relative, came quickly, and together they tried to lift him, but Thatha was too large for them. The relative ran out and got someone on the street to help them carry him into the car. They put him in the back seat, but his legs stuck out the door. They pulled them inside and closed the door. Sita sat holding his head in her lap.

They drove as fast as they could. Minutes passed, and Thatha continued to spasm.

"Don't leave me," Sita said, her voice breaking.

Thatha's eyes turned to her.

"Stay."

Thatha blinked.

"Stay with me, I don't have anyone."

"S—" he hissed.

"Don't leave me yet. You'll have many afterlives with your Satya," Sita said.

"Promise," he gasped.

Sita burst into tears. The car had reached the closest hospital. A stretcher arrived, and they took him inside. Doctors applied pressers, and Sita heard the cardiovascular equipment beeping. She stood, unable to help.

The doctors told her to wait outside. Sita obeyed. A rumble broke through the hot silence. Sita looked at the sky.

Drops began falling, one on her head, two on her shoulders, several on the yard in front of her. The earth drank them up as soon as they landed, but they kept coming. Within minutes, the drops had turned into a steady rain.

It was raining when Thatha appeared with an umbrella in hand to take her home from school. It had continued to rain as they walked, her hand in his, as each drop fell to the ground and threw a circle around itself.

It was raining inside the story too. The giant was drenched and lost in the jungle, looking for his son. He cried for his son, louder than the rain, and the jealous rain god cursed him to be a tree. It continued to rain when the giant, now a tree, spread out his branches, aching to touch with his rain-soaked leaves anything that might be his lovely son.

It was also raining the year before, when Sita had come to see Thatha and gave him the wooden cane, and he'd held it with two hands as if it were the body of his lovely son. It continued to rain down her cheeks when he went inside without realizing she'd come home at all.

And now it rained outside the hospital, when Thatha was desperate to join his son and leave her for good.

The next morning, Sita woke up in the waiting chairs outside the ICU. Thatha was still alive, for the time being. He'd had a stroke and now was being treated for pneumonia. He could go either way, the doctors said.

She walked to the hospital window. Outside, the sun was up and burning. Summer showers, by nature, were short. They punctuated the long season, marking the change that would come. But summer was not yet over. Like crickets buzzing in the trees, like laughter in the distance, like a sunset turning grass golden, like buffaloes ambling their way back from the pond, like Thatha counting out her age to the exact day, summers would always exist. Thatha would too. He had to.

The nurse called for Sita. They had changed Thatha's clothing and gave her his shirt. She'd seen him wear it over the years. It smelled of him, like coconut oil. Like home. She held it in her arms the way Thatha might, as if it carried the soul of a loved one. As if, deep inside the shirt—if she and the whole world kept quiet—she might be able to hear his heartbeat.

Lunch at Paddy's

Padmanabham clasped his hands to his chest when he found out what happened. Vikas, his twelve-year-old son, had invited a white boy to their house for lunch.

"He's coming tomorrow, not today," Vikas said, but the shock remained.

Paddy took off his work bag and plunged into the sofa. He turned to Latha. "When did you find out about this?" he asked his wife.

"He told me an hour ago," Latha said.

"An hour ago!" Paddy said. He hadn't expected this one bit. It had been a month since they'd exchanged their small town in India for a small town in the States, as he joked in the office. The move had been rough on the kids; they moped around the house and cried a fair bit, and so he'd advised them to make friends in school. The advice was no more than a day old; he had assumed Vikas and Niharika would befriend desi kids first and then slowly branch out. None of them knew how to survive more than five minutes of conversation in English, let alone an entire meal. And now Vikas had signed them up for this test.

Something was not right. If a bug got resolved in the first attempt to fix it, the fix was likely incorrect. This was true of both programming errors and parenting errors.

"I don't know what they eat. What should we cook?" Latha said.

Paddy put his hands on his head. He didn't know what white people ate. He saw them eating things at work: cheese, fruit, cake, salad. But what did they eat at home? What did they like to have for lunch? What was white-people food? He had no knowledge of what constituted a salad. Was a salad more than an assemblage of leaves and vegetables? Rice wouldn't work. Once his office had gotten Mediterranean food catered, and he'd watched as each of his colleagues transferred exactly one spoonful of rice onto their paper plates from a bowl he could have finished all by himself. And they'd said the food was spicy. It was bland.

"If you called me as soon as you knew, I'd have asked in the office," Paddy said, glaring at Latha. What could they do now?

Latha adjusted her pallu. "Why can't you call your friends now? All you do is sit down and google. Even the other day, I told you to stop and ask for directions. But you never listen. You fiddled with the GPS, and we missed the first twenty minutes of the movie."

"You can't do that in this country!" Paddy shouted.

"Can't you talk without shouting? The neighbors can hear us."

"Stop." Vikas waved his hands. "It's my fault. I shouldn't have invited him."

Paddy lowered his voice. "Come here."

"Don't worry, I'll tell Mike not to come." Vikas stormed toward his room and slammed the door shut.

"This is your fault," Latha said, proceeding to the kitchen.

Paddy suppressed a sigh and walked toward Vikas's room. Out of the corner of his eye, he saw Niharika hunched over a book. Normally a good sign, a hum of approval should have reached his chest, but his daughter was too mischievous to be unaware of the outside world, and he resolved to see what she was up to after he spoke with Vikas.

The door to Vikas's room was locked. "Open the door," Paddy said.

No response.

"I'll rip your skin off if you don't open the door now."

Vikas opened the door and fell facedown on the bed. Paddy asked him to sit up. When Vikas didn't move, Paddy sat on the bed and turned him with force. Tears slid down Vikas's cheeks.

"Why are you crying? You cry if something doesn't go your way?"

Paddy told him that lunch with the white boy wasn't a problem. Vikas should listen to his father and trust that he'd come up with a solution. Paddy asked about Mike. Why hadn't he told him about this new friend?

Vikas stopped crying and explained that he'd asked Mike to come over that day after math class. Paddy couldn't focus on what his son was saying; he didn't like that he'd had to make an effort to stop the boy from crying. Even Niharika, two years younger, didn't cry as often as Vikas did. Paddy had seen enough of the world to know what it did to sensitive types. He wanted to toughen Vikas up a bit, but Latha kept interfering whenever he tried. And the move had complicated things. He'd promised them that America was a welcoming place, that they'd have a great life. But what place doesn't have its challenges?

Vikas asked him something, if something was okay, and Paddy said of course, unthinkingly. Then he parsed what Vikas had said. His son had lured the white kid over by asking if he wanted to play *Call of Duty*. So now Vikas would become addicted to video games, and worse, the white boy would stick around after the meal.

Paddy asked Vikas, "Do you know what he eats?"

Vikas shook his head. "Sandwiches?"

Paddy clasped his hands. Where would they learn to make sandwiches now? Back home people ate bread only when they were sick. Even if they bought a loaf at the store, what would they put in the middle?

Paddy made his way to the kitchen to speak with Latha and stopped at the sight of Niharika scribbling something furiously. "What are you doing?" he asked.

Niharika continued to write in her notebook. "Nothing." It was never nothing with her, she was always up to something, but Paddy let it slide; he would deal with her later.

In the kitchen, Latha cut onions and chilies in preparation for a curry. Paddy remembered the last meal she'd prepared for guests before they left India. She'd taken offense at his suggestion that they get a couple of curries from a takeout to ease some of the cooking burden during the chaos of the move. "What's the point of life if you can't cook a simple meal for guests?" She'd made spinach dal, eggplant chutney, mutton keema, sambhar, and a plateful of sun-dried and deep-fried plantain chips. Everyone had raved about all of it and asked when they'd get a chance to eat her food again. Now there was a guest coming and her dishes were of little use.

"What curry are you making?" Paddy asked. He'd told her about white people, hadn't he? They'd gone to an Indian restaurant in town and asked for the food to be spicy but still ended up with food so bland they spat everything out. Had she forgotten that?

"Is the white boy coming? Or no?" Latha sprinkled red chilies in the pan.

Vikas stood next to Paddy and said, "His name is Mike."

"This is too spicy. White boy will die and his parents will sue us," Paddy said.

Vikas said, "Stop calling him 'white boy.'"

"I'm not stupid. This is for us," Latha said.

"Of course the white boy is coming. Why won't he come after Vikas invited him?"

"His name is Mike!" Vikas shouted, and left the kitchen.

Latha turned up her hands. "I don't know, I thought you canceled it."

"Have some sense, how will it look if we cancel after inviting?" Paddy said.

"Why don't you figure out what to cook instead of lecturing me?"

Vikas yelped from the hall and said that Niharika had kicked him in the legs. They each held half a notebook when Paddy found them.

Vikas turned to Paddy. "She wrote down everything you said today."

Niharika had transcribed all their conversations, right down to his threat to tear off Vikas's skin if he didn't open the door. She'd even heard him reassure her brother. Between the lines transcribing his reassurances, she'd written, *Vikas: sobs {like a baby}*.

Paddy kept his jaw firm and said, "What's this?"

"I was testing my auditory range," Niharika said, her eyes darting sideways.

Vikas shook his head. "Why are you spying on me? Why can't you be normal?"

"I didn't even move. It's not my fault you were crying when I was doing my experiment," Niharika said.

"Bullshit."

"What's that language, Vikas?" Paddy brandished his finger. "What did I tell you?"

"She says the f-word."

Paddy ordered her to their bedroom. Niharika didn't have a room of her own. She had always slept next to Latha, and this arrangement had worked fine until they gave her brother the second bedroom. And she began acting up. No doubt, her fight with Vikas had its origins in that. From the look on Niharika's face, Paddy knew the fight was far from over. But he was tired, his shoulders ached. He hadn't even gotten the chance to take off his watch after a long day of work. He stretched his back and yawned.

He reached for his cell phone to call a friend and ask what they should cook. It'd be silly to bother anyone late on a Friday night, he decided. He googled *what to cook for white people*. Casserole came up a lot. What was a casserole? He clicked and scrolled through pages of food. Five minutes later, he was no closer to understanding it. Pasta seemed easy enough. Latha could try one of those YouTube recipes.

He took the laptop to her. "How about pasta?" he asked.

"What's that?" Latha said as she stirred the curry. They had never heard of it before.

Paddy showed her a YouTube video. They'd have to go to a store and get pasta and cheese and the tomato sauce, but they'd be able to do it. Latha interjected. She didn't want to overcook the pasta; she said that the cooking times posted in the videos were never accurate. Why couldn't they just cook something she knew how to make?

Paddy grew exasperated. All she could make was Indian food. But then he realized that wasn't true. Latha knew how to make noodles. She'd occasionally made noodles back home. Long white noodles with chili flakes and soy sauce and the tiniest hint of masala. Indo-Chinese style. She could make them without the chili flakes, and they'd taste fine. He had seen colleagues buy Chinese food for lunch; white people liked Chinese food.

A look of relief passed between them. They'd cook noodles; the dilemma was over. Thank God for Chinese food!

"We don't have any noodles," Latha said, opening the steel container full of pulses.

At the grocery store, Paddy found so many brands of noodles that he had to call Latha.

He examined a noodles packet as he spoke. "Which one should I get?"

"Maggi," Latha said.

"There's no Maggi here."

Latha tut-tutted. "No Maggi? Did you check properly?"

Paddy wandered the aisles. "I already checked."

"Ask someone. Why wouldn't there be Maggi?"

Paddy shouted into the phone. "Because this is America!"

Latha sighed. "Okay. Get something that looks good."

"Looks good how? It's noodles on every package."

"I don't know. Just get something."

"I told you to come. You should have come here," he said, and hung up the phone.

Paddy chose a pack and went home. By the time he got it to Latha, he was told there had been a phone call.

"The white boy's mom?" Paddy clasped his hands. How had she known their number? "What did she say?"

"I don't know, I can't understand their language."

"Did she call to cancel? What's not to understand?"

"I don't work outside, how would I understand?"

"Oh God, what did she say? Why didn't Vikas speak?"

"Vikas was in the bathroom, so I said, 'One minute,' and gave the phone to Niharika. Go ask your daughter." Latha scrubbed the pan with fury.

Paddy shouted for Niharika.

Vikas came out of the bathroom. "Did you get the noodles?"

Niharika popped her head in. "Yes?" she said.

"Did you speak with Mike's mom?" Paddy asked.

Niharika made a song out of a yes.

Paddy grew suspicious. "What did she say?"

"She wanted to speak with you. I told her you were out."

Paddy clasped his hands and pulled them to his chest. He'd picked up this gesture somewhere. There was something about it that felt both performative and reassuring. It made him feel safe. "Did she say she'll call back?"

"No." Niharika's head disappeared into the bedroom.

Paddy had a feeling there was more. "She didn't say anything else?"

Niharika's head appeared again. "Oh yes, there was something. She said she's coming too."

"What?" Paddy clasped his hands again. "Now? Or for lunch tomorrow?"

Niharika shrugged with a tinge of a smile. "Tomorrow, I think."

Latha rushed from the kitchen. "Do we have to cook for her too? What will she eat?"

"Something very spicy," Niharika said.

"She said that?" Latha asked.

"I'll hit you with a stick if you don't say right," Paddy said.

Niharika said she hadn't understood everything, but the white lady had said something about dropping off her son. Then there had been a pause, and the lady had asked if her son could be dropped off at home after the meal and that she'd talk about it with Paddy when she dropped off Mike.

Paddy gulped. Lunch *and* a driving test? His driving was okay, but he tended to rely on assurances. If the GPS told him to take a right, he confirmed with whoever was in the car that he needed to turn right, a habit that arose out of his distrust of the GPS and a general fear of cops. He didn't want to jeopardize his status in the country by committing driving mistakes. The boy's parents could sue him for putting the boy in danger, and that'd be the end of their life here.

At night, after Niharika and Latha slept, Paddy kept imagining all the ways in which the lunch could go wrong. The white boy would likely ask him questions, and if Paddy was unable to understand, he'd look like a fool in front of his kids. Or the noodles could be too spicy for him. Or he could have an allergic reaction to something. He googled *what allergic reactions a kid has for food*.

He gazed at Latha sleeping, unworried, and wished he could do the same. He'd do his best to talk, to make the lunch a success, but what kind of small talk was expected of him? If Mike were an Indian boy, he'd have asked about his parents, where they came from. He'd have built a socioeconomic profile of the family with that information. In this country, he had no idea what coming from any particular place meant. He had a hunch that such questions were not welcome. And the more questions he asked, the more he'd have to work to decipher the boy's answers. But if he stayed quiet during the lunch, wouldn't that be perceived as an insult? It felt like one of those impossible coding challenges he'd had to do in job interviews.

Latha stirred in her sleep and asked him what they'd do if the boy said he didn't like noodles. He said he didn't know. Maybe they should learn how to make other Western dishes.

"You learn to cook first," Latha said.

Paddy was surprised at her tone. "What will you do then? Speak with the white boy in English?"

"Your English isn't that great."

"At least I'm speaking. I'm not gesturing yes and no like a villager."

Latha shushed him: "Niharika's sleeping."

Paddy left the bedroom and sat on the sofa. Latha didn't know how things worked. She didn't know how to navigate these situations, and neither did he, but that was somehow his fault. Maybe other Indian families would know what to cook and what to say. Maybe there was something wrong with him, his brain had an error built into it, and this was the best he could do. After an hour of googling *things white people say,* he fell asleep on the sofa.

The next morning, Paddy woke up to the sound of a spatula hitting the wok.

"Why are you cooking so early? The food will get cold by the time the white boy arrives," Paddy asked Latha.

"Oh, I didn't know that."

"No need for sarcasm so early in the morning. Are you planning on using the microwave to reheat the food?" They'd never had a microwave in India, and Paddy felt that it made the food worse.

"No, I'll make it again at eleven thirty," Latha said, chopping an unwieldy onion in the wok with the spatula. She was doing a test run. It had been a while since she'd last made noodles; she wanted to try again before she cooked for real.

In the hall, Vikas played *Call of Duty*. Also testing out, his body language conveyed. Paddy normally would have ordered the boy to study, but he let it go. He left the house and looked at it as a white person might, then walked through the hall observing the shoe rack, the corner lamp, the sofa—the necessity and location of everything. The shoe rack needed to be pushed closer to the wall. The photo frame appeared a little tilted and Paddy straightened it. He picked Niharika's books off the carpet and made her vacuum the floor. But the house still smelled like a restaurant. He grumbled about how much rent they were paying, and they didn't even have good kitchen exhaust.

When Paddy changed into his jeans to go to Walmart for scented candles, Latha bellowed from the kitchen, "We don't have any tongs."

"So?" Paddy shouted from the bedroom.

"Buy them now," Latha said.

"Why?"

"How would it look if we used a spoon to put noodles on the boy's plate and they spilled on the table?"

"Oh."

Paddy felt his chest tap like a woodpecker; he'd felt this way since he'd come to the States. It was a low-grade anxiety that coursed through his veins all the time. He had no idea America would turn him into such an anxious wreck. But what mattered was that the kids would have a good future, and Paddy took consolation in this fact.

He heard Vikas and Niharika fighting in the hall and walked toward them.

Vikas hit Niharika on the shoulder. "Why did you do that?"

Niharika laughed. "Piss, pish pish pish."

Vikas moved to strike her again, and Niharika blocked his hand.

"What's going on?" Paddy shouted.

"She lied on the phone," Vikas said, his eyes turning moist. "She ruined everything."

"What did you do?" Paddy turned to Niharika.

"I didn't do anything," Niharika said.

"She told Mike's mom I pi—"

Niharika laughed.

"Shut up," Paddy said.

Vikas continued. "She told Mike's mom I peed in my pants! That I couldn't come to the phone because I was washing them—"

"What?" Paddy shouted at Niharika. "Are you out of your mind? Don't you know how important this is?"

Niharika stared at her feet.

"Answer me. What did the white woman say? Are they still coming?"

"She laughed. It was a joke!" Niharika said.

Latha rushed from the kitchen. "What? Is the lunch happening or is it canceled?"

"Yes, almost." Vikas went to his room and slammed the door behind him.

"No, it's not, he's overreacting," Niharika said.

"What did you do?" Latha asked Niharika.

Paddy gripped Niharika's shoulder. "I'm asking you for the last time. Is there anything you've not told us?"

Niharika shook her head. "There's nothing. I swear I'm telling the truth. They're still coming."

Paddy clasped his hands in relief. He dragged Niharika to the car. He had no time to scold her at home; they needed to get the candles and tongs. Back in India, he'd have given her a slap or two. In this country, he'd be arrested for something like that. A friend had told him that. When he told Latha how ridiculous it was, she'd said, "You better control yourself." As though he couldn't discipline the kids otherwise.

On the way to the grocery store, Niharika leaned against the window.

"Why? Why did you behave like that?" Paddy asked, his voice low and fierce.

Niharika continued to look away. She looked on the verge of tears.

"Are you crying?"

"Never."

Paddy was confused. "You could have just not told Vikas. You could have waited for your joke to arrive with the white boy. Why did you gloat and pick a fight now?"

Niharika shrugged.

"Ah!" Paddy said, tapping the wheel. It was because she was jealous. She didn't have any friends. Nothing for her, everything for her brother. Maybe programming errors were simpler to fix. He didn't know the answer, but he held on to the hope that the lunch would solve everything: first her brother, then her.

"You'll be fine," Paddy told her.

Niharika stared ahead. "I'm excellent."

"You'll make friends at school soon enough."

"I have fifty friends. None of them are racist."

"Good," Paddy said.

At Walmart, Paddy reached for a flyer that advertised a sale on dishes. He dialed Latha to ask if he should get some extra china in case the kids brought over multiple friends without notice. Latha felt that they should purchase kitchenware that wouldn't break, and Paddy surveyed the sale items until he ran into his colleague John.

"Hey, good to see you, Paddy!" John waved.

Paddy introduced Niharika to John and said they lived close by and then headed down the aisle with a "See you Monday." He felt pleased about the exchange.

As he put the scented candles in the cart, he noticed that Niharika had disappeared. He found her by the soda, grabbing a bottle of some kind.

"Good idea," Paddy said. He hadn't thought about drinks. But Niharika had something other than Coke in her hands.

"What's that?" Paddy asked.

"I don't know, I want to try it," she said, holding it tight. "Can we please get this?"

"Is that alcohol?" Paddy clasped his hands.

"Yes." Niharika nodded, turning her face away from him. "Ginger ale has more alcoholic content than this, but I think this is a good place to start."

"Enough!" Paddy snatched the bottle out of her hand and read the label: TONIC WATER. "It says water."

"Tonic. It's diluted alcohol, good for kids."

"I don't believe you," Paddy said, and pulled out his phone to google it.

"You trust Google over your daughter?"

"Shut up," he said, typing, *Is tonic water have some alcohol?*

Niharika giggled.

Paddy ushered her in the direction of the checkout. "I'll hit you if you don't behave."

"Please don't." Niharika laughed as if she knew he couldn't.

Paddy looked at her. She'd never done this sort of thing before. In the past, she'd always apologized when she'd misbehaved. He'd kiss her forehead and she'd turn back into a sweet, bookish girl, but now she was laughing freely, without a pinch of fear, as if he were the village joker and not the engineer who worked hard to give them a better future. He grew angry for the first time in a long time. He'd never been truly angry—how could he be mad at his child?—most of his anger had been a necessary drama he put on, and this time would have been no different but for her merciless laughter. He sensed that by moving the kids to a country where he didn't know anything, he'd weakened his own position as a father. The only way to get past this loss of authority would be to exercise control, and so he glowered at her as a reminder of the punishment that awaited.

"You just wait until the white boy leaves," he said.

Noodles steamed hot and slender in the wok. Cutlery rested on white place mats on the dining table. Candles spread aroma, fake rosemary. The carpet bore faint vacuuming lines. Paddy showered and put on his most flattering shirt. He'd come up with a fail-safe strategy, something project managers did to keep the developers going. He'd ask a couple of questions about the boy's hobbies and find a way to compliment him. If he had to drive the boy home, he'd ask if he enjoyed the video games and tell him that he was welcome back anytime.

Everything had been arranged. Nothing had been left to chance. Latha sat on the sofa by the window. Niharika peered from the bedroom window. Vikas stood on the porch. Paddy paced the courtyard. Every few minutes a car passed by and he froze in the direction of the car, then stretched his shoulders as if he'd intended to do exactly that. He posed questions at the sky. What car did they own? What job did the mother have? Nobody knew.

Twenty minutes passed and there was no sign of the boy. Sweat glistened down Paddy's forehead and he began to take deep breaths.

Vikas drooped over the porch. "I don't think he's coming. I was stupid to think he'd actually come."

"They're just a little late," Paddy said, drawing him close. "They'll be here."

Vikas ran inside, and Latha followed him. A white woman biked down the street and Paddy watched the spokes turn. He'd thought people were punctual in this country, unlike back home. Surely they'd turn up ten minutes later with a story about car trouble. He sat on the curb watching a bird hop down the road.

Niharika came and sat next to him. "They are so late."

Paddy didn't respond. She was trying to apologize, and so he didn't look at her. This was key. He had to remain grim and unyielding. A squirrel ran across the street.

But he couldn't help himself. "How are you so sure I won't hit you?"

"Auditory range," Niharika said, touching her ear. "I heard you telling Mom."

Paddy raised his hand. "Doesn't mean a thing. I'll still hit you. You can go live with white people."

"There's a car coming." Niharika pointed.

He stood up to welcome the guests. There was no car.

Niharika burst into laughter. "I'm sorry," she said.

He caught her wrist. "Do that again, I dare you."

"I said I'm sorry," she said, wrenching away. "I was angry, that's why."

"What?"

"What's wrong with Padmanabham? Paddy sounds like a rice bag." Niharika put on a fake American accent. *"Good to see you, Paddy."*

He understood she was parroting his colleague John. Was that why she'd caused trouble at Walmart? Stupid girl. "Paddy is easier to pronounce," he said. "You don't know anything."

A vehicle in the distance, a tall one, too big to be a car—a truck?

"Are you going to introduce yourself to that kid as Paddy? Because that'll be weird."

That's right, a kid, he thought, clasping his hands. It was just a kid coming. This boy was only the first in the series of white boys who'd come over for lunch, and this was only the first of many lunches at their house. They were in America, after all, weren't they?

A moving truck lumbered past.

"You better go inside before I hit you," Paddy said to Niharika, pacing again.

She turned toward the house.

"Let's all wait inside," Latha shouted from the porch, her

palm holding a weeping Vikas's head on her shoulder. "You can come back out when they get here."

Vikas continued to weep. Niharika walked up to them and threw her arms around Vikas.

They looked at him from the porch. As though he had dragged them to this country and left them standing on the street.

The bird on the road took off and landed on a tree.

He prowled back and forth, looking for the shape of a white boy. Any minute now.

Sunday Evening with Ice Cream

The distant tinkle of bicycles comes to me like the scent of hydrangeas from our flower bed, the air infused with a lilting ardor. I quickly wash my face and sit on the stairs facing the street. A motorcycle snarls past aunties in red and lilac sarees. I brush the dirt off the sleeve of my salwar kameez. The boys haven't arrived yet, the tinkles still faint and few.

Radha leaves her house across the street and walks toward me in a blue churidar, her face powdered white. She's heard them too.

Water drops slide onto my cheeks. People know their angles, their faces, how they look best—my best face is a wet one. In the bathroom mirror, the pores on my nose close with a splash of cold water and my cheeks glisten with a luster I wish I had all the time. A few minutes after the wash, it's gone.

By the time Radha sits next to me, my face has already dried. I can feel my pores enlarging again, my nose probably fat as hell. I consider telling her I need to pee, but she'll know that I left to wash my face again, and so I remain seated.

Radha holds out a candy. I take it and say, "You smell nice." It's a pretense, not that she smells good or bad or like anything at all, other than the baby powder she wears to mask her pimples. But that, for a moment, I'm not thinking about the boys who will soon cycle back and forth down our street, I'm not waiting for a boy to transform my face—that's the pretense.

The chirps of bulbuls perched on the telephone pole linger in the air. I can hear Aunt Chaya sweeping inside the house, the rhythmic scraping of the broom. She is my father's sister, younger by eleven years, though she hates being referred to as his little sister. "I'm my own person," she'll say to the offenders (when my father isn't there), and leave the room with a twirl of her saree. But the real issue is that my father has always been the kind of person naturally drawn to socialization, the de facto mayor of the revenue department, receiving a constant stream of visitors after he comes home from work, and with my mother being long gone, Chaya is forced to supply the visitors with endless rounds of tea.

"My mom is making mutton curry," Radha says.

"What's the special occasion?"

Radha shakes her head. "Nothing. Just like that."

Voices, bells, laughter. Radha stiffens. "Don't look, they're here."

The bells peal louder, and the voices grow looser, laughter now a chorus.

I continue talking as if I haven't heard them, as if I care only about what Radha has to say. "So, you asked your mom for mutton and she's cooking it for you?"

Radha's eyes pivot back to me. We've played this game before where neither of us explicitly notices the boys, but both of us know from the occasional glance which ones have come and which ones have looked at us the most. I tuck a strand of hair behind my ear loosely enough that I can do it again and again, tilting my head at an angle in which my nose can be viewed and not thought ugly.

"Yes," Radha says, more distracted than usual. She's been getting a lot of one-ring calls on the telephone in her house, but the call always ends before she can pick up.

One-ring calls are the rage right now at Little Flowers High School. If you have a crush on someone, you copy their landline number from the eighth-grade attendance register and give a short ring, precisely one, and then you hang up. You do this three times in quick succession. Since it's mostly boys who do this, boys who aren't allowed to speak with girls at school, it becomes a guessing game as to who isn't taken yet and who has a crush on you. If you get four one-ring calls on the same night, that's as serious as it gets.

I trace where Radha's eyes have been. There are six boys with bikes—Vicky, Suman, Rahul, Dinesh, Chaitanya, Adil—all taking a water break in that fortuitous spot, fifteen feet away. I go through the boys like they're a selection of dolls. Radha has an eye on Vicky, who disembarks and leans over his bike as if he were adjusting the chain, but really he's looking at her.

"Don't look." Radha tugs at my wrist.

"I wasn't," I say.

"What's up with you today?" Radha asks, worried that I'm giving us away. I'm less experienced than her at this. Radha knows how to present herself in a way that leads to interactions outside of school; I don't. I'm more bookish than her, and for the longest time I've been deeply oblivious to Strike, a different game, one everybody else plays in class. The rules of Strike are simple. It starts when it becomes apparent that someone is checking out their crush. You count the seconds until they look at the other person again. Fifteen seconds or forty seconds or two minutes or however long it takes, the shorter the interval the more interesting it is to watch. When the glances are reciprocated and the eyes meet in a perfect match, you shout, "Strike!" I didn't understand why people kept shouting "strike" so often until I saw the girl next to me blush. Then it became obvious, all those looks. I get the stray glance or two, but I've no real admirers. No one-ring calls, no looks, no strike.

"What's up with *you*?" I ask, referring to the way her eyes keep darting.

Radha smiles a little. "I saw him yesterday at the market. I can't tell if he followed me."

"Who, Vicky?"

"Shush! He'll hear you."

"Let him listen."

"No, I mean," Radha says, her eyes still jumping around, "I was just curious why he was there last night." She sneaks a glance and turns to me, flushed. Which means they're approaching.

"So, about the mutton, did your mom fry it? What's the recipe?" I ask.

Vicky slides his bike next to us. The other boys join him. We exchange awkward hellos.

Vicky smiles at Radha. "Your dress is nice."

Radha giggles, and the boys snicker. None—really, none of them—are looking at me. There is nothing I can do about my nose, but I touch it all the same. Everyone spins their heads, monitoring for adults who would put an end to this right away.

Radha says, looking at Vicky, "I saw you at the market last night."

"Ca-carrots," Vicky stutters. "My mom sent me to get them."

At this, the boys burst into laughter. Vicky turns to them: "Why are you laughing? You haven't done any errands, fuckers?"

Radha laughs, but I wince at how easily Vicky swears. No one in my family swears, and I'm unused to the way those words allow you to say things without meaning them. It makes me feel naive, sheltered. Like I don't know what a man can do to a woman. I want to know how someone can make me anew, but it'll have to be the right man. Not these boys.

It gives me comfort to think that I've rejected the boys and not the other way around. And once I begin to believe it, I can feel how right I am. Vicky hasn't grown any facial hair yet, and it's common knowledge that his mother wipes his mouth after he drinks milk. Suman bites his nails all the time, and when he brings chocolates to class on his birthday and passes them around, his fingers are so gross I'm too disgusted to eat the chocolate he drops in my hand. Dinesh is (a) shorter than me and (b) of a lower caste; any interest in him could only be temporary because my father would never allow for anything more—that would be a scandal for everyone involved. Rahul, on the other hand, belongs to the same caste and his family gets on well with mine, and yet still, there's something awful about him. Not just him, but all these boys. They go after girls who are fairer or have noticeable breasts. I resolve to stop caring about any of them.

"Aarti, are you done with the math homework?" Rahul asks me.

Six sets of eyes on my face. "Yes," I say, tucking my hair.

"Can you lend me yours?" Rahul smirks, and everyone laughs.

The implication that I, as an academically motivated girl, am only of interest to the group if I let them copy my work, pulls me back into the game. I decide to be cool. "What will you give me in return?"

Oohs.

"Two rupees," Rahul says. A fizzle of laughter.

"Twenty and we'll call it a deal."

"For twenty rupees, you can bribe the teacher," Vicky says to Rahul. Laughter again.

The streetlight flickers on, casting the long shadows of the boys and their bicycles but also lighting up Rahul's thin-mustached face. From this angle, he doesn't seem half-bad.

"Is Uncle home?" he asks, referring to my father. All eyes on me again.

"No," I say. There's no telling when my father will come back in the evenings. Often much later, but sometimes as early as seven, with a bunch of associates who will talk and talk. By then the group will have disbanded, but something tells me I'll be revisiting this little interaction with Rahul over and over again all night.

The conversation moves on. Vicky asks Radha if she's ever gotten any love letters. Directly. Radha blushes, and everyone else laughs nervously.

"No," Radha says, her eyes down and with a little shake of the head, as if she doesn't know how such a thing has never happened.

"You can tell us," Suman says. "We won't tell anyone."

Vicky stares at Radha.

Radha shakes her head again. "No one's given me anything."

"How is that possible?" Vicky asks.

Radha laughs, and Vicky produces a folded letter from his pocket.

"Here, take this."

The boys cough in unison: *Ahem, ahem!*

"For me?" Radha takes it.

"It's a blank page," Vicky says, and laughs.

I groan. Radha moves to give back the letter, nostrils flared. "Keep it in your pocket."

The boys cackle. The front door opens behind me and Aunt Chaya walks toward us. "What's going on out here?"

The boys spring onto their bicycles and pedal away furiously. Gone in an instant.

Radha stays next to me, crumpling the page.

The folds of Chaya's nightie brush against my back as she stands behind me and peers at the street. Ignoring Radha, she looks to the left, then to the right, sees nothing. Then she glares at me. "Shouldn't you be studying?"

"I'll come in five minutes. Go back inside," I say, looking away from her.

She leaves, saying, "Of course, why would you respect me? I'm just the idiot who threw aside her life to take care of you." Her regular refrain. Chaya had just finished her MA in English at the University of Hyderabad when my mother ran away with one of my father's associates. It was a big scandal. My father and his friends found them in a hotel, somewhere far from here, and beat up the guy. But in the end my father gave my mother up because she, according to Aunt Chaya, told him shamelessly, in front of everyone, that she was in love with the other man, that she wanted a divorce, that she was happy to let him have full custody of me.

After that, people mocked my father behind his back: he was a cuckold. Chaya came home to see how I was doing, to console her brother. She'd gotten on the overnight bus and arrived to the sight of my father struggling to feed me. I wouldn't take it; at four, milk was poison to me. Chaya, though, somehow knew what to do. She fetched a small plastic spoon and dipped it into the glass of milk, saying, "One spoon, you won't die from one spoon," and stuck it in my mouth. Ergo, problem solved, she thought. But solving that problem would lead to a much bigger one. My father looked at her with so much wonder and amazement that she knew immediately—she was trapped.

She couldn't possibly abandon her family in their time of need; she might have, if only she hadn't seen that look of desperation in my father's eyes, if only she hadn't picked up the spoon. Her life became our life; she left everything behind, but for one friend from university whom she keeps up with on the phone. And so, I don't have the right to say anything to her, and neither does my father, who gradually regained his position in society by virtue of having a family that supplies visitors with snacks and tea. I doubt my father would ever say anything mean to his sister; he'd brought forward numerous matches for her over the years, exclusively from our caste, but she'd refused all of them: "This one is too short," "That one is too tall," "I can tell just from the picture, this guy is dumb, his PhD is probably fake." My father would protest that she was being unreasonable, but that'd be the end of the matter for a couple of months. As I grew older, the pool of qualified grooms became shallower and shallower, and soon my father stopped trying because Chaya was, as she said, "too old for that business." If she hadn't been so picky, she could have found someone.

Once Chaya is out of earshot again, Radha asks, "What's her problem?"

"You know her," I say. Chaya might have gotten a better match, one she might have agreed to, if she hadn't belonged to our scandalous family. Maybe that's why she was so bitter. There were rumors at one point of a lost love in her past, when she was at university, but when I asked about it, she bristled and said,

"What nonsense," as if she'd never stoop to falling in love, wasn't the kind of person even to consider it.

"I can't imagine what it'd be like to be unmarried forever," Radha says. "The things people say. I'd have married an idiot like Vicky."

I chuckle. It's the exact thing I want to know. "So, you'd marry him?"

Radha giggles. "I mean no. But who knows what'll happen in the future?"

I can't wait any longer. I ask, "Did Rahul make a pass at me?"

"He totally did!" Radha laughs. "Why else would he ask you about your father?"

"Oh, his father is friends with mine. I think they've been here together once or twice."

Radha hums as if that could explain it. The croaks of a frog briefly turn my eyes to the narrow roadside canal, strewn with plastic waste, that runs adjacent to the houses on the street.

Across the way, Radha's brother shouts for her. She leaves with an easy gait that I imagine must come from knowing she has admirers, boys who are so thrilled to call her that they don't even need to speak with her. I sit alone for a moment longer and listen for the bulbuls, but they're long gone.

The telephone rang once and stopped. I find myself standing near it, breathless. Was it a wrong number or a one-ring call? I sit by the phone; it doesn't ring again.

When Chaya asks me why I haven't showered yet, I grudgingly leave. In the bathroom, I strip and look at myself. Black-heads all over my squab nose and pores open like the gates of a temple. I set about squeezing my nose, digging the blackheads out with my fingernails. Hold, squeeze, scrape. My nose turns so red I can't breathe. I release my grip and inhale and wrestle again. Hold, squeeze, scrape. It's been only a few days since I've done this, and I'm convinced my face was made to attract dirt. If I stand next to Radha in the street, pollutants freed from the exhaust of a speeding motorcycle will levitate in the air for a second, lost and exhilarated, and shoot toward me, completely ignoring her, as if I were the only one present, as if I spoke to them personally, as if I whispered in their cells, "Come to mama."

I roll my hair into a bun. Water pours from the tap into a bucket; we don't have a showerhead. Radha had told me in passing the day before about shower fittings that haven't made it to our town yet—how they shoot water at your face, how if you aren't careful, you can get your hair wet when you don't want to. As I retrieve water from the bucket in a plastic mug and empty it over my body, I think about what being in love with someone (Rahul?) would mean. Would my body lose track of individual senses? Would I stop seeing water on my skin, stop smelling the chlorine in it, stop hearing it pat down my body, stop tasting it in my mouth, stop feeling it soap my body—and just sense it breathing in every molecule of my being?

Chaya knocks on the bathroom door. "Are you sleeping inside?"

"I'm done," I yell. I rinse and clean up.

"Open the door." Chaya bangs again. "Can you hear me?"

I get dressed and open the door as slowly as possible.

"What were you doing in there?" Chaya shoves me out, saree in one hand, and locks the bathroom door. I understand: Father is bringing home guests. She can't serve them tea in a nightie.

She has to abandon *Mansfield Park* or whichever big fat Jane Austen novel she is rereading at the moment and shower and change into something presentable.

The phone rings and stops. Goose bumps flare on my arm.

It rings for the second time not long after, and I pick up right away. There's no one on the other end; the person (Rahul?) has already hung up. My heart pumps rapidly. I stand by the phone waiting for the third call. A whole minute. Nothing. But just as I step away, it comes. The third and final ring. He's no longer a question mark; he's definitely interested. Butterflies take wing in my stomach, each flutter strumming in me a song of inexplicable joy.

I imagine a direct call sometime later. Chaya picks up the phone expecting her Hyderabad friend, whom she talks to for hours and hours, but instead it's Rahul, asking to speak with me. She reluctantly hands the receiver to me and stands close enough to hear what I say.

I pick up the phone and ask, *Who's this?* as if I've multiple lovers.

Rahul, he says.

Yes? I say, looking past Chaya staring at me.

I was joking about the math homework.

I know.

Smart girl. I just didn't want you to think that I couldn't handle a simple assignment.

Can you?

I can.

Really? I say, a slight inflection in my tone.

Yes.

I'm not so sure about that.

Give me a chance, he says, and my heart plinks down the receiver.

"What are you giggling about now?" Chaya interrupts my daydream. She's standing outside the bathroom; she's finished showering. I'm grinning like a pig.

"Nothing. I remembered a joke," I say, reaching for my chemistry textbook.

Chaya goes back into the bedroom. "Study! Or you'll become a laughingstock."

I sit in my usual spot between the living room and kitchen, leaning against the wall, from where I can see, except for Father's bedroom, all the rooms in the house. I open the textbook and pretend to read. I get distracted thinking about a recent Sunday evening, when Rahul yelled, "Frog!" at Suman's feet and the boy fell off his bicycle in confusion. It had struck me as immature at the time, but now it feels extremely funny.

On the page, the organic structure of ethanol. Blah. I turn from ethanol to Chaya. The bedroom door is still open; she's putting on a chiffon saree. She measures with her thumb and index finger and forms pleats in the front. She tucks in the drapes and begins holding the saree to wrap around her jacket. Chaya clearly has decided to look her best tonight, which she does every once in a while when she's bored of wearing the same old things. On fancy nights, she always unlocks the almirah and uses her expensive moisturizer. She never lets me use the moisturizer, which of course only makes me more determined to get some. I close my book and approach her.

She turns to me, pin in her mouth, the fold of saree in her hands. "You're done with studying already?"

"I'm taking a break," I say, trying to sound jokey.

She shakes her head as if to say, *This girl*. I hover around her as she pins the top of the saree to her jacket.

"I know why you're here," Chaya says.

I sit on the bed. "I just want to see it, okay?"

Chaya takes some talcum powder into her hands. Has the moisturizer already been used? I get up and inspect the shelves.

"It's not there. Don't think about it." Chaya brings her hands to her face and neck.

"My face is all dry!"

Chaya briefly holds my chin and looks at my face and moves away. "You're fine."

"Why can't you let me try it?"

"Do you want me to tell your father?"

I glare at her.

Chaya looks at herself in the mirror. "Once you go down that route, there's no turning back. You need to become a doctor. What's the point of all my effort if you don't even study? Go study!"

I stare at her chiffon. "Is the district collector coming over or what?"

Chaya sneers. "I can't even make you give tea to the guests. My brother will ask me why I'm putting his child to work." She sighs. "It's my fault. I should have married some guy and left you both, then you'd have realized how much I do for you."

I grow frustrated. "Why don't you marry Uncle Ramesh and be done with it?" Among my father's associates he alone is a Dalit and he alone isn't married.

Chaya freezes. She doesn't like most of my father's associates because they see her only as my father's sister. But Uncle Ramesh she dislikes because he pays extra attention to her. He also studied in Hyderabad and seems to pride himself on a sense of his own civility, that he's better than us townsfolk; he greets her enthusiastically, tries to help her pick up empty teacups, and even gives her the Reader's Digest he picked up in the city. He shows excessive deference, which Chaya says is the sign of a man waiting to loot you.

"You just say whatever floats into your head?" Chaya raises her hand as if to hit me.

I duck and run away laughing. I've let my mouth run and I like where it's gone. I wonder if this is how it feels to swear. I feel powerful. Like I can say anything. I can be in love with someone (Rahul?), and my father will get us married because I'll know exactly what to say. No one will think to compare me with my mother.

Chaya shouts from the bedroom: "I'll tell your father."

And just as quickly as it had come, I feel my power recede, not because she'll tell on me, not because I'm afraid of my father (although I certainly am), not because I regret what I said (although I certainly feel bad about using Uncle Ramesh as a stick to beat down Aunt Chaya), but because in all of my surge, I still can't bring myself to fully believe that Rahul is interested in me or that I actually like him. He's still a question mark and maybe will remain one forever.

The gate clinks open and I hear several voices. The bickering laughter of grown men. My father and his group. I run to my books to appear as if I've been studying. My bun comes loose and I put a clip on it. Chaya heard the voices too; she rushes to the kitchen to heat milk for the tea. I take a pencil and underline the principles of esterification and saponification. The creak of kitchen cabinets opening and closing slides softly in my ear.

Ten minutes later the phone rings again. By the time my father reaches for the receiver, it stops. I jump up from my spot, panic all over my face.

My movement catches my father's eye. "Aarti! Come here," he says to me, introducing me to the visitors. The stench of cigarettes, from one of the guests, overpowers the slightly woody aroma of anise and cardamom in the tea. I trace my left ear with my hand and hold the books against my chest as I stand in front of the visitors.

Hari Prasad, Ramesh, Suryanarayana—I know the regular uncles. They work in the revenue department with my father. The one thing I know about Suryanarayana is that his distant cousin was accused of hacking his own daughter to death for marrying a Dalit man. Beside him now are two new men. One of them is bald, except for around the ears, and has a package of some kind in his hands, wrapped in a plastic bag. The other has a large belly like a politician's.

Father holds my elbow while he speaks, looking at the bald man. "Do you know who that is? Uncle owns a dairy farm outside of town."

The phone rings again and stops before Father answers. (*Rahul, please stop, okay?*) "Weird," Father says when no one says anything. My heart pounds so loudly that I'm afraid Father will hear it. The uncles talk about me, but I don't try to follow which one of them is saying what: "She's going to be a doctor. Class first in her school." "Very good." "You have to make your father proud." "No question. She will be a doctor; she will bring great respect to her father."

Father beams and pats my elbow. I turn to slip away when the bald man speaks.

"Girl, take this ice cream inside." He holds his package out for me to take.

"Why, sir, no need." My father shakes his hands, smiling.

"It's straight from our dairy," the bald man says. "You all should try it. Try it now."

My father gestures toward the kitchen. "But my sister is making tea."

"Take this box inside and bring a small quantity in bowls, just a little bit, and we'll taste it," the bald man says. "Let's taste it."

Father asks the guests, "After tea or before?"

"Now."

"Before."

"Definitely now."

"Won't taste good after tea."

"No."

"Will spoil the after-tea taste."

"Yes."

"Get only a little bit."

"Small quantity."

"No more than two spoons."

"Tiny bit."

In the kitchen, I find Chaya muttering to herself: "Not just tea, but they also want ice cream in bowls. As long as there's someone to give them food in bowls they don't have to wash themselves, they'll have it all. Why not?"

Chaya lowers the heat on the stove to a simmer. She takes the ice cream from my hand and sets it on the countertop. I steer clear of her and go to the bedroom.

I lean against the bed frame and spread open my textbook. My thoughts turn to the fourth phone call. (He's that serious about me?) To ease the lingering anxiety in my mind, I write my name and Rahul's name in the margins of a notebook, telling myself I'm not that kind of girl, I just have to see how our initials look together. I keep doodling them and striking them out while I listen to the men talking about Obama, the new American president, whether he'd give any money to India, before joking that if their acquaintance Papa Rao went to America, he'd talk everybody into electing him president. Boisterous laughter.

I peek. Chaya is handing them ice cream. Uncle Ramesh gets up to help. Chaya, clearly irritated with him, insists on handing the bowls out herself. They're all half-full and the men complain that it's too much, but they eat it all nonetheless.

Someone knocks at the door. "Aarti!" Father shouts.

It's Radha. She's come in her pajamas, her hair loose and wet like she's just taken a shower. I meet her at the flower bed. The phone calls have instilled a new confidence in me; I've no anxiety about Monday or the chemistry quiz. The sight of hydrangeas and bougainvillea and ferns in our flower bed land gently on my soul, and I speak cheerfully. I smile, gesturing toward the guests in our living room, some of whom can be seen through the front-facing window: "I wonder if this is how all boys behave when they get old."

Radha glances at them and back at me, her head swiveling all over the place to make sure no one can hear what she has to say. "I called, but I saw the guests and thought it'd be easier if I came over and told you in person."

I stutter, "*Y-you* called?"

"I know, I'm lazy." She laughs. "I'd have just walked here, but I had oil in my hair. I tried calling you before I took a shower, but my idiot brother kept disconnecting the phone. He had to make an urgent call or something. Useless."

I feel weak; I bend down and straighten my pajama folds. That close to the flowers, I can't smell the hydrangeas. I want to bury myself in the dark soil under the plants, but there's nowhere to hide. I rise.

"Anyway, it wasn't a blank page," she says, her eyes radiant.

"What? Oh, the letter Vicky gave you?"

She produces the letter she'd crumpled earlier. "Read it," she says, giggling.

I open it.

> *Dear Radha,*
>
> *Ever since I first saw you, I've wanted to tell you that I've lost my heart. I'm telling the truth, you can ask anyone. The moon pales before your beauty. If you don't believe me, throw away this letter, but please don't show it to principal sir.*
>
> *If you like me, touch your ear three times in class. Waiting to see u again.*
>
> *Faithfully,*
> *Vicky*

I give it back to her, forcing myself to smile.

Through the window, I see Chaya serving tea to the guests.

Radha pokes me in the shoulder. "Why aren't you saying anything?"

"I'm happy for you," I say, trying to keep a poker face even as I'm drowning.

Radha blushes. "It's the start of a new headache, I guess. Do you think he'll want me to do the ear thing right away?"

I shrug. As Radha continues to chatter, I feel myself slipping away. What sickens me is that my standards are so low. I could have been convinced that almost any boy was calling me, and I'd have kept up the same pretense; I'd have been fine with any boy who wanted me first and allowed me to want him back, and not just because I've no idea how to open that door to my life, but also because I fear that deep down, truly fear, that even if I did open that door and wait patiently for someone to pop in and say hello, I'd find that there's something so rotten inside me that people passing by could smell it, a peculiar sourness that would keep people away, reducing me to books and exams and grades, sentencing me to a life of questioning, wondering why no one ever dares to look at that open fucking door.

"Hey, still there?" Radha waves her hand in my face.

I can't pretend anymore. "I have to sit," I say, sitting down on the series of bricks that separate the flower bed from the cement floor.

"What's wrong?"

"I thought it was one of the boys calling me." I try to smile. I feel ashamed to admit it, but I've no one else to talk to. And the thing comes out of me before I can turn it into a joke.

Radha laughs, taken in by the way I grin, and then cottons on to what I've said. "Oh," she says. "Oh. I'm sorry! It was my stupid brother—"

"It's fine." I grin again. But she doesn't buy it.

She sits on the bricks next to me. I look at the guests laughing, at the teacups in their hands, at Chaya standing behind the pillar—at something other than Radha and the pity on her face. Radha says she really did think that Rahul was interested in me. And I hate myself for having told her the truth. I must have looked even more embarrassed, because she changes tack and tries to cheer me up by saying that it's only a matter of time before someone falls for me but stops when I force a smile and tell her it's fine, really.

She snaps a bougainvillea flower and smells it, takes apart the petals, and says, "You know, we're still in school. Who knows what'll happen when we're eighteen?"

I don't respond, but it strikes a chord with me. There's still plenty of time for me to grow a bigger chest, a shapelier body. I've time. I'll even have a husband someday—maybe not the one I wanted, but someone who'll have me.

Chaya walks in our direction, holding two bowls of ice cream, and I'm ready for the consolation of dessert. She hands one of the bowls to Radha and the other to me. Radha's has a steel spoon; mine, a plastic one.

"Why did you give me a plastic spoon?" I ask.

"Be happy that I gave you anything at all," she says, turning back. "All the steel ones are in the sink. I don't have a maid to wash dishes for me." Makes sense: I'm destined for leftovers.

Radha licks her spoon. "Look at your aunt."

Chaya is behind the pillar, listening to the conversation, smiling.

Radha continues, her tongue numbed from the cold of ice cream. "She looks happy. And that's after turning down so many matches."

I keep eating, wishing Radha would stop so I can focus on the melt in my mouth. "Girl, stop. I'm fine."

Radha laughs. "Wait, look. This sounds crazy, but I think your aunt is giving someone secret looks. She must be so horny, she's eyeing the guests. Look, look."

"Shut up," I snort. But I look over at Chaya and see that it's true—she's making eyes at the guests from behind the pillar, holding the kettle, listening to the conversation under the pretext of supplying more tea. Just as usual, poor Chaya, alone on the outskirts. I feel a sudden kinship with her.

But as I watch, the pattern emerges. Her eyes keep darting

to the far right. Five seconds, look. Her eyes become luminous. Thirteen seconds, look.

"Are you seeing what I'm seeing?" I ask Radha.

Radha turns to me. "Who?"

"The uncle on the far right."

"One . . . two . . . three . . . four . . . five . . . six . . . seven, strike! One . . . two . . . three . . . four . . . five, strike! Your aunt is on fire!" Radha grows excited.

Chaya moves from behind the pillar to collect the teacups, and Ramesh gets up to hand her his. Strike! It's then that I understand: Ramesh is unmarried, he too has studied in Hyderabad, Chaya speaks for hours with her "Hyderabad friend," she dresses her best when he comes to visit, she knows guests are coming even though my father never bothers to give her a heads-up, she never shares her moisturizer that he must have given her as a gift (I think?), and she never submits to any pressure to get married. I feel unmoored. Chaya isn't just an aunt, she's a woman, a woman who's held on for years to a love she can never have, and I'm still a child who knows nothing. She can't abandon her family, can't give up her love, can't risk meeting him alone, can't let us catch on to how she feels, can't reveal what rages in her mind; she can only give shape to what cleaved her heart: a love affair conducted with nothing but the light in her eyes.

Radha turns to me. "Can you imagine being in her place, loving someone secretly all your life? This is so crazy."

It's clear to me: I'm never going to be this woman. I'll become a woman someday, but never this woman. Neither will Radha, with her stupid boy who cares more about getting caught by the school principal than writing a letter so impassioned that Radha would have stowed it away in her bra and not shown me at all.

Even if I end up finding someone, I can't imagine loving them from a distance. With as much devotion. I will never be able to love like that; I'm too rational, too fixated on my own happiness. Radha is in this too—our lives are nothing compared with Chaya's. It's hard to think about the future, but I'll have a husband, a family someday. And so will Radha. We'll have long meandering lives, all pulp and action like a fruit drink—sometimes satisfying, sometimes comforting, but always predictable, always artificial. We'll have rich husbands and fancy showerheads, but we'll never know what it's like to be so passionately in love. We'll have thousands of Sunday evenings, some of them with ice cream and plastic spoons, but we'll never know the fire of this single Sunday evening (November 9, 2008), which will be lost to us forever. We'll know the scent of hydrangeas and we'll know the chirps of a bulbul, but we'll never know the sound of a hydrangea or the scent of a bulbul—because five senses are five senses for us, each distinct and lovely and comfortable and expectable and lonely. We'll never be the people to throw an entire life at the sight of a face, but we'll always be the plastic littering the streets.

Next to me, Radha continues to count: ". . . nine . . . ten . . ."

The Protocol

He climbed the four little stairs outside McDonald's and felt it: this, this was where he'd meet his first wife. Soon, he'd meet the Black woman and marry her and divorce her and pocket the green card. She'd chosen the location. They'd spoken on the phone and agreed to meet before the city hall signing.

Her text arrived: *I'm here.*

Little kids pattered out through the door, and he stepped inside. He dithered around the soda station, trying to determine which woman was Ashley; he felt a tap on his shoulder. Braids topped up like a gopura, beads around her neck, earrings the size of lemons. She wore a white T-shirt that said ZERO FUCKS GIVEN.

It was not how Gautham had imagined he'd meet his wife.

Gautham was from Rohtak, a small city in Haryana with far fewer women than men, one of those places where masculinity ran like drain water on the streets. When he first arrived in America for a PhD in biotechnology, he'd had certain expectations. On the plane to Boston, he'd seen a series of raunchy comedies and concluded that American women were loose, and blondes particularly so. He fantasized about having sex with a blond woman and later amended this fantasy to include a small clip of them marrying each other in the local Hindu temple, because he felt guilty for taking advantage of the woman's loose-ness and having sex before marriage.

But when the semester began, Gautham realized that no white woman would even sit next to him in class, forget mar-rying him. He'd decided white women weren't his type. A tra-ditional Indian woman who cooked and cleaned and touched Ma's feet when they went to India, sure, why not, but he'd grown up watching Bollywood films with songs, tears, and col-orful weddings. He'd imagined he'd spot his fair-skinned desi woman one romantic, wintry evening at a party or a temple. Sparks would fly, and cue the duets and the grand finale. But then he'd graduated, found a job, bought deodorant, hit the gym, scrubbed his privates, shaved on time, ironed his shirts, spiked his hair, dressed nicer, and the damn woman hadn't shown up. What did, though: bald spots. And bad luck. His H-1B visa application to work in the country hadn't been picked in the lottery system. He had only a few months in America before he'd be forced to stand outside Ma's door. Unless he secured a green card.

The chatter inside McDonald's rose: a pack of teenagers in hoodies and sweatshirts swung through the door.

Gautham looked at Ashley. She was young, early twenties. He'd never thought he'd marry a Black woman. He himself was dark-skinned, but if he married a woman darker than him in India, people would treat his children even worse than they treated him. They'd shake their heads, lampoon them: *What can you do? You got your mother's color.*

The teenagers dragged chairs and formed a large table.

"How did you know it was me?" he asked Ashley.

"Look around," she said. There weren't any other Indian men.

He felt dumb—this was a recurring thing. An inability to

understand and navigate American social situations. He called it dumbness, the feeling of being a cow amid humans. He'd developed a strategy to try to contain it, similar to what you do when you need to fart in public. Hold it in for a little while and it passes.

They sat down at a table that smelled of chicken fingers and ketchup. Gautham offered to get Ashley something and was relieved when she refused. An encouraging sign—hopefully she wouldn't milk him for more than they'd agreed upon.

"Do you live around here?" he asked.

Ashley stared at the glass exit. "When I was like five, yes. There used to be a bodega across the street."

Gautham nodded his head and smiled; he was happy to have understood her. In his first semester, he barely understood the guy working in the campus cafeteria, the first Black person he'd interacted with. Chicken sandwich—did he want the onion raw or caramelized? The question was a simple one, but it eluded him completely. Twice more, the Black guy asked, the people behind waiting. He wrapped his head around the sound of those words, and the Black guy shouted something and sent him off to the side. He'd left the cafeteria humiliated.

"So how do you know Ajay?" Gautham asked. It was Ajay, his colleague and friend, who'd set him up. Ajay had arrange-married a Black woman, Ashley's cousin, and sent her half his paycheck for two years, the time it took for the permanent green card to arrive. "Imagine sleeping with the knowledge you won't be kicked out of the country. You can change jobs, you don't have to worry about being picked in the visa lottery system and then having to wait twelve years, or more, for your green card. You could own a Dairy Queen or a gas station; you could sponsor your mother's visa. The possibilities are endless," Ajay had said, his mustard teeth showing. Except for the part about sponsoring his mother's visa—Ajay didn't know anything about Gautham's relationship with his mother—all the other possibilities he mentioned seemed ripe.

Ashley's phone beeped and she pulled it out. Gautham's eyes fell on the screen. The wallpaper was a photo of a baby girl. Was Ashley a mom? That seemed like something he should have been told before they'd met. Convincing the green card interviewer that he'd married a single mom, and a poor Black woman at that, out of some intense love wouldn't be easy. The photo on the phone, the baby girl, better be a niece.

"Sorry, I was just checking to see if Nia was okay. I left her with a friend," Ashley said. "My daughter," she added.

"I didn't know you had a daughter," Gautham said. "Ajay didn't tell me."

"I don't know why he'd know. I've never met him. My cousin had an arrangement with him." She stared at him. "Is there a problem?"

"If you have a kid, how can I marry you?"

"What?" Ashley put her hands on the table.

"I don't see how this will work—with a kid." Gautham pulled out his phone. Where could he find another American citizen to arrange-marry now?

"What's my kid got to do with it?"

"How will we convince the green card interviewer that the marriage is real?"

"I don't know what you're so worried about. You don't even have to fucking talk. My cousin told me what to say. We come up with answers to a list of questions and I say them. Even if they don't believe it, they can't call bullshit unless *you* give them a reason." Ashley stood up.

Gautham shut his mouth. It felt jarring and unpleasant to hear the f-word in the mouth of a woman. She was confident, this lady. It was wiser to go along with her. He put the phone back in his pocket and said, "Please, I need this to work, or I'll have to leave the country."

"Okay, look," Ashley said. She sat down and closed her eyes. "If I didn't need the dough, if I didn't have all these fucking loans, if I didn't have a daughter to take care of, I wouldn't be sitting here, not for one second, okay?"

It angered Gautham that Ashley spoke to him like that. But he sensed she'd spoken to him, like Ma, out of necessity. Ma had given up on him long ago; she'd dealt with him because society had demanded that of her. She spent all her time at the Congress Party office, organizing campaigns and building a political career, coming home only to sleep. Sometimes he'd run into her in the kitchen, and he could tell what she was thinking: how simple her life would have been if he hadn't been born. If he'd at least been a girl, she would have married him off as soon as he got his first period and washed her hands with bleaching powder. But he wasn't a girl, and so her house was his home, he could come and go as he wanted and there wouldn't be any questions; he was to be fed and tolerated, but even when he was endlessly polite and studious, he was still nothing more than the retching image of a father he'd never met.

Something about the way Ashley sat, body facing the door, gopura leaned back, eyes closed, was deeply familiar. He knew then—she was speaking the truth. This was someone who wouldn't go near him if she didn't have to. She needed the money; she was tolerating him. He didn't know what to say, he felt it rise—the onset of dumbness.

On the day of the city hall signing—Gautham didn't want to think of it as his marriage day—it rained and rained. Water pooled in the streets. He woke up, sat on the toilet, jumped in the shower, and tried to remember where he'd last seen his umbrella. He had only one suit, which he'd bought for job interviews, and he couldn't afford to ruin it in the rain.

He didn't know what the appropriate etiquette for a wedding like this was. Wouldn't he have to kiss the bride? What was the proper kissing etiquette in these sham marriages? A kiss on the cheek or a peck on the mouth? Could they refrain from kissing altogether? Ashley would be horrified to kiss him. He'd leave it to her. This kissing business was a Western thing, less of a surprise to her; she'd know what to do. On a different day, he could have zapped off to the fantasy of being asked to kiss a woman, and who knew what was next, but today he needed to move. He put on his pants and looked for the umbrella in his office bag, in the closet, under the bed—it was nowhere to be found.

Gautham held a plastic cover over his head and ran to the CVS near his apartment. By the time he returned with an umbrella, Ajay had arrived in his used BMW. Gautham put on his blue suit and banged his foot into the bathroom door and howled and hopped into the car.

"Hey, marriage boy," Ajay said, moving the camera sitting on the front seat to the back.

"Did you have to kiss that woman?" Gautham pulled the strap over his shoulder.

"You and I will be relatives, sort of. Can you believe it?"

"Did you kiss her?"

"I got you a wedding photographer." Ajay pointed toward the camera and laughed.

"Listen, did you kiss your ex-wife?"

"I didn't pay for that." Ajay twirled his mustache.

"In the wedding, you idiot, did you kiss her?"

"Oh, ha, we just held hands and hugged."

Gautham exhaled. The car wipers were fast at work sweeping away jets of water molecules. In less than an hour, he'd marry a woman with a child. A woman with whom he had no chemistry, no love. It wasn't supposed to have been like this, but he'd take it. Something meant to get him where he needed to be.

They parked the car and walked inside, sharing the umbrella. Ashley sat on a bench, pretty in a white dress. Not the kind of fancy wedding dresses he'd seen in movies, just something cheap, no frills, simple. He smiled at her.

"How's Nia?" Gautham asked.

"She discovered the existence of *Candy Crush*," Ashley said.

"It's a fun game," he said, and they both smiled. He'd never played the game, but here he was, making conversation. A sudden burst of energy found its way into his suit.

They marched into the clerk's office and the marriage court was empty. They didn't find anyone for a few minutes, and Gautham feared it wasn't going to happen. But twenty minutes later, it did. They held hands, looking at each other, but the magistrate's pen wasn't working, so he pulled out another from the bottom drawer of his desk, and Gautham glanced at Ashley's lips when she turned to look at the magistrate, and the wall clock approached 11:10, and they said the marriage phrases sweet and crisp, and Ajay clicked ten pictures a second, and all of them put on a synchronized performance of smiling faces and signing happy hands, and soon they were grinning and laughing, and Gautham and Ashley were legally pronounced husband and wife.

"You may now kiss the bride," the magistrate said, and bent down his head to conclude the paperwork. Gautham and Ashley moved into a hug, and Ajay took the pictures that they'd later use in the application as evidence of their relationship. The occasion got to them, and they hugged for a few seconds longer than expected. Right then, in each other's arms, and for the foreseeable future, they were married. Husband and wife. There was a moment in the hug, Gautham felt, when relief spread through their bodies, he could feel it in the way Ashley's fingers clamped his back, in how she was a warm, natural fit in his arms, and in the manner in which he felt her smile, osmosis then and there, for once a genuine smile seeping into his heart, and he knew, somewhere in the hug, there was a moment he could have kissed Ashley and she would have gone along.

The protocol had been agreed upon a long time prior. With phones and the internet, there was no reason to meet in person. On the first of every month, until the permanent green card arrived, Gautham would deposit $2,500 into their joint account, and Ashley could spend it however she pleased. They'd text each other to confirm the transaction. Twice so far, he'd texted, *Deposited the money,* and Ashley had replied, *Got it, thanks.* She couldn't ask him for any extra money. The rule was necessary even if Ashley didn't seem like the kind of person who would do that. Any documents shared for the application were to be kept confidential, and their personal lives weren't to be disturbed in any way.

He knew the implications, but it was still a surprise when he held a hand to the morning sun and opened the mailbox outside his apartment. Forget the big corporations, how did the neighborhood grocery store find out her new address and know to send her coupons? He'd added her onto the apartment lease and car insurance and health insurance. One of those bastards had sold the information, and so, despite her not actually living with him, he was getting twice the junk mail, and he had no choice but to empty the mailbox daily.

Gautham ripped the mail and put on his boots. At work, he read green card interview experiences while computations ran on data sets in the background. There was something called a Stokes interview they must not get, a horror of a secondary interview where everything was questioned. Couples were separated and asked to draw a map of their house, identify which key goes where, and reveal the brand of condom they used. Their best bet was to go through the standard interview without raising doubt. He printed out a list of thirty questions someone on the internet had gathered and shoved it into his bag when no one was looking.

Gautham had to stand on the T home. His reflection appeared in the train window, and he touched his hair. It was thinning faster than roads back home—he had to find his woman before it was all gone. He stood clutching the handle, observing people around him, mostly women in low-hanging dresses, short skirts, short shorts. Opposite him was a party of six college students. An assortment of thighs. He couldn't stare at them, but he could do what other people did, which was to wait and look and then appear to contemplate a mystery beyond the legs. What he got out of it, he couldn't say. Back home, people would stare, and he'd be free to stare alongside them. As though by staring you could understand what those foreign bodies were made of, what lay underneath the tank tops, how firm were the breasts—was the skin color lighter in those parts? Why does anyone wear shorts so short the tight underside of their butt hangs out? But on the T, he just peeked. And it rose in him, the desire to know. It frightened him, the intensity of this desire. He was on a train—what if it showed?

He shut his eyes and prayed to Hanuman and chanted all his various names to cool it down. Every night he'd coax it out of him, let sleep rid him of it, but by morning it woke his blood afresh. It was beyond reason. If Ashley or the women on the train knew what he was thinking, God never, they'd jump out of their bodies. *Asshole!* they'd scream. They'd lunge with their handbags and cell phones—*Creep!*—they'd shove him in jail—*Pervert!* As if it were enough. As if he were a piece of shit but human nonetheless. As if he deserved to exist at all.

"What does your mother-in-law do?" Ajay asked, reading random interview questions off the internet on his phone.

"She's a social worker." Gautham peeled an orange. He'd never meet Mrs. Jackson, but he knew where she worked, and he had a photoshopped picture proving their common interest in baking cookies. "Next," he said.

"What side of the bed does Ashley sleep on?"

"Left. I go for the right." Gautham put an orange segment into his mouth. Ashley had taken that one in their Q&A Google Doc. He'd entered his family information and she'd entered hers, and they'd each taken a stab at the questions. Ashley would do all the talking at the interview, but if they got pulled aside for a fraud interview, God forbid, his answers shouldn't give them away. But he had faith in Ashley; he knew she'd do a good job. The way she'd written some of the answers, he felt like he understood her personality.

What did you recently celebrate?
G: I recently got promoted to Data Engineer II. We celebrated by having dinner at Sitara, an Indian restaurant.

Who cleans the house? Who cooks?
G: I cook and Ashley does a lot of the cleaning. (Is this okay?)
A: ok.

What challenges does your spouse face at work?
A: racist patients. toxic nursing chiefs. mean doctors. let's not fucking go there.
G: I'm sorry to hear about the racism. My manager (white) keeps mixing up me and Girish, who is a foot shorter than me. I'm asked to train data sets at very short notice and the management puts a lot of pressure on me.

What do you two have in common?
A: we are very similar in who we are. we have the same values. we believe in hard work, and family, and respecting each other's culture. our love is built on mutual respect.
G: Beautiful answer 😌
A: thank you

What are your hobbies? What do you like to do together?

G: I love watching cricket. I'm a big fan of IPL (like NFL). We both like watching TV and going on walks. (Ok?)

A: I'm getting into knitting. *Insecure* is my favorite show.

G: Is that on Netflix?

A: HBO

G: I will check it out.

What do you like the most about your spouse?

G: She is fun-loving and adventurous. She will try any dish I make. (Ok?)

A: i like many things about him. he's a careful planner. always keeps track of what i need. when we go on a road trip, he will plan a stop at Wendy's and get me curly fries. but the thing i like the most about him is his ability to learn and improve as a human being.

G: If the interview goes well, I will get you curly fries. ;)

What's your spouse's favorite food?

G: Biryani. I like everything chicken.

A: mac and cheese

What bothers you the most about your spouse?

A: if i really think about it, the one complaint i have is that he will see me putting dishes away and continue watching his cricket instead of helping out.

G: She occasionally makes fun of me for not knowing things. Once she let me believe that if I take a

hundred quarters to the U.S. bank, they'll give a
dollar extra, $26 in cash. (Ajay did this to me!)
A: lmao

Do you leave lights on when you go to sleep?
G: No.
A: i do! Nia hates darkness.
G: Can we say No (or Yes) and not mention Nia?
G: Ok?
A: ok

There weren't many questions after that. Gautham had continued to refresh the Google Doc for a couple of days even after
they stopped working on it, as though he'd expected the conversation to continue in some capacity, new responses to old
comments or new doubts that had risen from existing answers.
He searched the internet for more questions and decided
against adding them to the Google Doc—the ones they had
were sufficient.

"Relax, man. You don't have to know all this," Ajay said, putting down his phone.

"Your ex-wife wasn't a mom," Gautham said. But he knew
Ajay was right. Most interviews were straightforward and often
a formality.

Ajay gazed at his phone. "All right, answer this one. What
position does she like? Missionary?"

Ashley had talked about respect, and this felt wrong.
Gautham threw the orange peels in Ajay's face. "You got your
card, so what do you care, man?"

Ajay laughed. "Chill, you'll get it too."

Ajay's phone rang. It was his wife, and Gautham could hear

her voice leaking into the air. She wanted to know when Ajay was coming home, and could he bring some olive oil on the way back, and she was bored, could he come now? Ajay stepped away to talk, and Gautham began wondering about his second wife—where was she, when would he meet her, when would he lie next to her? After Ajay got his green card, his parents had set him up with a girl and he'd married her and brought her over to the States. Ma wouldn't bother. She was more interested in her political career than in being a mother. He'd have to find his own bride.

From the balcony, he heard Ajay shout into the phone. He was shutting his wife down, telling her not to nag. He dawdled back inside a minute later. Gautham asked about his wife, how she was adjusting.

"She doesn't know anything here. She gets a bit lonely when I go out." Ajay shrugged. "It takes time," he added.

Gautham collected the orange peels and threw them into the trash. If it were him in Ajay's place, he wouldn't leave his wife alone in the apartment. He'd be in bed with her all day. He'd buy her a car, teach her to drive, take her out often, buy things for her, make her happy. He wouldn't yell at her, like Ajay did, and spend time away from her, helping friends. It struck him that Ajay wasn't doing this just for the sake of friendship either. Ajay cared about him, but he was far more important to Ajay in a different capacity. Who else could he talk to about living through his own fake marriage? The part of Ajay that had endured this thing, the part that had to remain a secret, the part that had overcome the immigration system and made him feel like a hero, it was dead without Gautham.

.　.　.

It was late October and pumpkins watched over the houses on Gautham's street. The T was three blocks away, two stops away from the station by the USCIS building where his fate would be decided. But Gautham had time; he decided to walk. This was the day he'd get his temporary green card—maybe not the actual card, but a confirmation of sorts. The arrival of success. He felt it in the way trees rustled, a gentle dance of branches, a leaf teased out now and then. He felt it in the way cars moved on the street, an aura of soft braking, jazz leaking, the occasional elbow out the window. He felt it in the laughter of kids in the distance, costumed and ganglike, running, flying, childhood gushing everywhere. Everything said, *Do not worry. Be her loving husband, hold her hand, and let her speak. Smile and get your card.*

He saw Ashley in front of the building, waiting for him. She wore a green dress, very pretty. He'd started watching *Insecure*. Should he say something about it? She saw him and waved. They entered the building holding hands, hers soft like a child's. He was afraid his palms were sweaty.

They were given a token number. He estimated a half-hour wait.

"How was your weekend?" he asked.

Ashley smiled. "It was good. I went to my mom's, got some sleep."

It took him a few seconds to grasp that she meant her mother had taken care of Nia while she got some rest. "Must be hard," he said.

Ashley shrugged.

Gautham moved closer and whispered. "Does your mother know about today?"

Ashley snorted. "Hell no. She has so much patience with other people, but she can't handle me."

"Same as my mom," he said, pleased to laugh with her.

"Maybe I'll change as Nia grows up, but I can't deal with that judgment, if you know what I mean."

Gautham didn't know what she meant. But he remembered what she'd written about respect and guessed that she wasn't being respected. "I know," he said. And he felt dumb for lying and letting those words hang in the air. He overcompensated. "I think you're an inspiration."

"Why?" Ashley looked surprised.

A security guard walked past them. Gautham stayed silent, as though he didn't want the guard to hear them, but he searched his mind for a proper response. "You're figuring out your life and helping mine," he said.

"That's so nice of you!" Ashley smiled.

"So curly fries tonight?"

Ashley stared at the screen displaying token numbers. "We're up!"

They hurried toward a room, where an elderly white man with glasses sat at his desk.

The interviewer asked them to speak only the truth and nothing but the truth. He examined their documents and entered case information into the computer.

Gautham glanced around the room, filled with framed USCIS paraphernalia. Questions were directed at the citizen sponsoring the green card; there wasn't anything for him to do. His eyes fell on the interviewer's hair. It was gone at the temples and thick at the top, unusual for a man of his age.

"When did you two meet?" the interviewer asked Ashley.

"Around this time last year," Ashley said.

"In Boston?"

"Yes, I was finishing up college and I was at a party, and his friend was in the same college, so he'd come to meet him, and we ended up talking."

The interviewer typed into the computer. Gautham was confident; Ashley was saying it as it had happened in his head. It was a beautiful fall evening and he'd had no idea there was a party. He'd come to visit Ajay and been ushered upstairs, introduced to some of his friends. Tina, Charlie, Ravi—he didn't remember the rest of their names. There were different kinds of pasta and beer and Coke and cigarettes and whiskey. In the corner of the room were dirty dishes stacking up; the floor pumped to the latest hits. He had a hard time hearing these new people, but it was fun, Friday night, and he was zipping. Ajay was in the middle of the room, dancing with an Indian girl. He didn't want to disturb him, but he had an urge to pee. He sashayed along the edges of the dance party, trying to find the bathroom. He stepped out of the room, and there she was, the love of his life. "Too loud in there," she said to him, looking like Ashley, and he nodded and said something in return, he can't remember what now, but it was definitely funny and flirtatious enough for this cute, sophisticated woman to give him her phone number. And then came coffee dates and movie nights and long drives and sleepovers and love bites and college loans and disapproving mothers and race be damned and one life is all they get and all they need is love and now their future was in this country so why not get a green card and here they were, Gautham and Ashley, happy and married.

How he wished it were true.

The interviewer asked Ashley a few more questions. Where did they live? What was Gautham's job? Did they file taxes together? Could he see some photographs? Gautham slid them out of the documents folder and gave them to him. He examined them all.

"Who's this?" the interviewer asked about a photo with Ashley's mother.

"Ashley's mother," Gautham said, and smiled, happy to be involved. The interviewer nodded.

"Do you have any pictures with your husband's family?"

Ashley said, "His family lives in India and they haven't approved our marriage yet, but we hope they'll come around." Ma popped into his head; Gautham pushed her out.

He peeked at his watch. They'd been in the room for a little over fifteen minutes. They should be celebrating any moment now. He looked at the interviewer, his thick hair, his blank face. He couldn't tell what the interviewer was thinking, but then he could never tell what Americans were thinking.

"Thank you for these." The interviewer passed back the photos and stood up. "I'd like to ask you both a couple of questions individually. Would you mind stepping out of the room for a while?" he asked Gautham.

Gautham's armpits turned into rivers. He stood up and left the room. This wasn't the Stokes interview—the letter in the mail requesting a fraud interview. One blog had mentioned this type of questioning as a possibility, but he hadn't found any records of such experiences. Maybe this was just an overzealous officer. Maybe he'd noticed a lot of green card marriages between Black people who could use the money and brown people with new tech jobs. Or maybe this: *Too many people of color in the country, send this bastard back, and if we're lucky and the marriage is real, we'll have gotten rid of two.*

Gautham stood outside the door. He couldn't hear a thing.

Two minutes later, Ashley came out and held the door open. Fear in her eyes. Gautham went in; this room felt much hotter.

"Your wife told me you didn't have a honeymoon."

On their Q&A doc, he'd answered the question about where they went for the honeymoon: *Because we have student loans, we decided not to go on a honeymoon.*

The interviewer smiled. "Where would you have gone for a honeymoon if you could?"

The most common of all questions wasn't on their list. He'd assumed their answer was enough, and he felt it creeping up— dumbness. His first impulse was to tell him they hadn't thought much about it, but what couple doesn't talk about taking a vacation? About going somewhere nice to celebrate their marriage, or at least talk about going somewhere down the line? If not a weeklong European honeymoon, a Marblehead one-night celebration? And more important, what had Ashley said to the guy?

Gautham felt bloated. "We didn't think much about it, because we have student loans—"

"Right, but if you could?" The interviewer leaned back in his chair. He was grinning.

Gautham repeated his spiel, but it didn't matter what he said; the guy's grin said it all.

Outside the building, they began walking in the general direction of the train station. They analyzed what had happened in the interview a dozen times, but they kept circling back, discussing what exactly was said. Ashley kept apologizing, saying that she should never have said Hawaii. Gautham refused to let her take the blame. The question wasn't fair, he told her. He'd wanted to name a place too, somewhere he'd have liked to go with his wife. If anything, it was his fault—he should never have left India. A country was an empty T seat; you should never leave in search of a better one. Once you go, there's nowhere to return.

The world hadn't changed in the past thirty minutes. They walked past the same sounds, children were still laughing, cars were still moving, and trees were still rustling. His whole life, he'd believed the world had an intrinsic quality. If submerged, the world of a person would sooner or later float up, lift higher bit by bit. But he understood now, he said to Ashley. "That's not how gravity works."

He had no idea what he was saying. Words he'd never spoken before flew out of his mouth, dumbness nowhere inside. "That's so true," Ashley said, striding alongside him in a deep meditative funk of her own. They walked beyond the train station, close to Gautham's apartment.

"So, what's going to happen? Are they going to send us a Stokes letter?" Ashley asked, continuing to walk.

"Or an outright denial." Gautham wasn't sure. "I need to research it," he said.

"The legal implications?"

Gautham had no idea, but he told her not to worry. Nothing ever happened to citizens.

Ashley said, "No, let's look it up now. Ugh, why is my phone so slow?"

They were one block away from Gautham's apartment and three from the nearest Starbucks. "Do you want to come up to my apartment, to research?"

She did. Here was finally a woman who wanted to come to his apartment, and it was his wife. In the lift, Ashley talked about her cousin who was dating a lawyer, and Gautham remembered how dirty the apartment was. There were dishes piled in the kitchen sink, and he hadn't vacuumed the place in months.

He offered Ashley the couch and sat on the chair he was using to hold up a space heater. Ashley asked for the Wi-Fi password. Gautham gave her his laptop. He searched the fridge for something he could offer: lemonade. He served it in plastic cups and felt he should have washed a couple of glasses and served it in them instead.

Ashley pulled her face out of the laptop and shook her head. "This is fucking crazy."

It was crazy all right. There was nothing they could do, except wait for a letter that informed them one way or another. Gautham didn't want to think about it. He wanted to be as far away from hope as possible.

The interviewer had said with a straight face, "You'll be hearing soon." How soon was soon? Ashley said, "I hope it's not next week." She told him she didn't want Nia's birthday to be clouded by anxiety. It was her third birthday and maybe the first the child might remember.

Gautham said, "Can I ask what happened to Nia's father? I don't want to intrude."

Ashley sighed. "I don't care. We broke up a long time ago. I haven't seen him in a while. He wasn't a good person. Sometimes I see him in Nia's face and it gives me the jitters."

"I grew up without a father," he said, without thinking. He remembered how his mother had been when he was young, always aloof and exhausted, and he wondered if being a single mother like Ashley had played a part in how his mother had distanced herself from him.

He told her about the time he went up to his mother as an eight-year-old and asked her if it was true, what the kid next door had said, that she didn't know who his father was—was there any truth to that? He'd only meant it as a can-you-please-tell-me-once-and-for-all-about-my-father, and she'd slapped him in the face.

Ashley patted his arm and said she was sorry.

She said a few more words, but he didn't hear. He was surprised by how things tumbled out of him. He went to the apartment window. It wasn't in the weather forecast, but it had started to drizzle.

"I can't believe we did all that for nothing." Ashley put her face in her hands. "What are the odds? One question. I can't believe I said Hawaii."

"Hawaii is a nice place," Gautham said.

"It is! I've always wanted to go there," Ashley said. "You said you wanted to pick a place too. What were you going to say?"

But then the drizzle increased, and Ashley looked at the window. She'd lost track of time, she said. She had to go home. Gautham offered to walk with her to the T, but Ashley didn't want him to get drenched.

Gautham got out his umbrella and gave it to her. She thanked him. "I'll give it back," she said, and hugged him goodbye. There was a moment before the hug, when Ashley said bye and unlocked the door but didn't open it, choosing to turn toward him instead. Somewhere in that moment, he felt his desire for a different world reflected in her, a world in which he could ask her to stay and she would.

Gautham locked the door and slunk onto the sofa. His eyes went to the lemonade cups, almost empty. Ashley had been here; these cups were evidence that, for over an hour, there had been a woman sitting in the apartment. His wife. And she had asked him a question about where they might have gone on their honeymoon if they'd truly been married. Where he once imagined he'd go with his real wife.

Switzerland: he was sitting in one of those fancy European trains with his wife, and they were looking out the window, going gaga over the mountains, the train chugging past rolling meadows and cute little huts and white cows that all looked up as the train went by. He had an urge to tell Ashley this, to answer her question; she'd probably laugh and say, "That's nice." He picked up the phone to call her, to try to make her laugh. He could ask her if she'd gotten home safely. He pulled up her number but stopped before he hit the call button. Not appropriate, he suspected. He felt it come, dumbness back in his gut.

The Math of Living

I've been working for the *Chicago Tribune* for about a year when it strikes me that I will go home in six months. The ticket has been booked and I'm ready. My boss has reviewed the JavaScript code and made his updates for the day. The code is in production.

I've been working for the *Chicago Tribune* for about two years when it strikes me that I will go home again in five months. The ticket has been booked and I'm ready. My boss has reviewed the JavaScript code and made his updates for the day. The code is in production.

I've been working for the *Chicago Tribune* for about four years when it strikes me that I will go home again in three months. The ticket has been booked and I'm ready. My boss has reviewed the JavaScript code and made his updates for the day. The code is in production.

Everything about my going home is formulaic. Plug in different numbers and I'm home already. Sometimes I think this is my legacy—not everyone can write themselves a home. I tell myself it's the next best thing to being on a plane.

Math of Living [i]

By the time this plane lands, I will have traveled for twenty-six hours.

This is not new to me.

The distance between the place I live and the place that lives in me is more than eight thousand miles.

Every hour of the journey home, I will look at my watch, even though the screen in front of me has a world clock. This is so I'm not fooled by the time zone changes. Every minute of the journey, I'll have the consciousness of going home. I'll try to forget it, to lose myself in a good book. But there is no such thing as a good book when you're going home after [x] months. I can't but sense where the plane is heading.

The plane will land and people will rise. There will be an extraordinary wait to get off the plane; men and women will argue about their place in the queue after retrieving bags stowed elsewhere. Then it will be over. I'll get through customs and exit the terminal. This is the moment I've been waiting for. My parents will be at the airport, waving at me from a sea of onlookers. They will be as excited as children. My father will do [a] or [b]. My mother will do [b] or [c] or [d]. It's not surprising that my parents will shower me with love. I know they can't help it; they haven't seen me for a long time. They will offer to take my bag and ask [e] questions about my well-being. I will feel the weather greeting my skin. At this point, I haven't gotten into the cab yet, but I don't have to reach the house to know the conclusion of this journey. I've already walked through the door; I walked through it in that moment outside the terminal. Home is the recognition of the lives we led together once, the things that only we knew of. It's the sound of the river that runs in our veins. Or rather, the shape of a story we tell ourselves. Who doesn't love a good river?

In the cab, my father will ask me either [f] or [g] before proceeding to tell me everything that has changed in the city since I last visited. My mother will ask [h] questions about the food I'd like to eat. I will enjoy this attention, this care that was missing when I was a child. It's inevitable that [j] minutes later, my parents will start quarreling. That's just who they are; they can't help it. I'll start feeling anxious; I'll never be as happy as I am in the moment I arrive. The magic will be over; all that's left, mundanity. I'll briefly feel like rescheduling the return flight I have in [k] days and going back to work. But I can't do that to my parents. Their faces are still glowing, and I wonder if love is a candle lit by distance.

The cab will stop at the toll gate that keeps increasing its prices. My father will take out his purse, but he doesn't have [l] rupees. I will have to pay for the toll. He will not look at me, the humiliation in his face transforming into anger. My mother will glare at him, the shine entirely gone. This is not new; I know there is no money. I must continue to work in a country that will never be mine for them to have something to eat. Poverty isn't anyone's choice. Some lives are meant to be. There's a Hindi idiom for this I cannot remember. If language is a city, mine is crumbling block by block.

The flight attendant asks me if I want [m] or [o], they are no longer carrying [n], and I refuse both before I realize what I'm doing. I don't call her back. I'm sick of airline food. And then, of course, I cannot escape the guilt; I'm exercising a luxury I hadn't known before. I take consolation in the fact that I will enjoy sumptuous food at home. Everything will cost [p] times less. I'll have [q] rupees to splurge at restaurants. Better to go in the first few days, before the restaurant money also goes toward our loan payments and household expenses. That's if the medical bills don't take away more than [r] rupees. Everything is a calculation. My father has often said to me, Why are you spending [s] dollars on a plane ticket? Why are you coming home almost every year? As if I didn't factor this cost into the math of living. I remember telling him once that capitalism has figured this shit out. That having a day off makes a worker more productive in the long run. Just don't kill me over a flight ticket, I might have said. But you can never please the math teacher in a father, the one who taught you to solve for *x* first, before you do anything else. The things you say don't add up. There's no mathematical value to feeling adrift in a white country.

Seat belt warning: turbulence. There are [t] babies on the plane and they are all crying. I put on the headphones and pick a movie. One of the teenage lovers has cancer and has [u] months to live; I'm not interested. I ogle at the house depicted in the movie; what I'd like is a spectacular home in which to die. I cannot stop working, I cannot abandon my people. My mother has severe bronchitis from years of exposure to heavily polluted air. I'd like to bring her to the country that has me by the collar, I'd like to say to my mother, *You gave me breath, and now, I want to help you breathe*. None of that is possible without money. And time. And work. And exile. What has exile done? It has taken everything I had in return for the idea of a home far, far away. Home is the sound of a river you are better off keeping at a distance. What else can you do except listen?

There's a voice in the cabin telling me I am [v] hours away. I know how this goes; each flight is more or less the same. This is the part where I wonder if my father was right, if I should have stayed in America. Guilt is what I have left after a lifetime of not acting on my desires. A rupee spent on a toffee is a rupee wasted, the ice cream that everyone is having is probably not good for me, *nothing* is always the correct response to *what do you want*.

In the cab, my parents will argue incessantly about the necessity of taking a cab. I cannot stand it; I will begin to wish that I'd saved the money and not flown home. We'll make do with [w], I'll assure them. My mother will cough from the dust creeping through the windows, and I will tell her I brought her American medicine, Tylenol, and she will smile. Anything foreign is good, and everything home is sickness. Haven't I been reading the news?

My father will ask me how I like America, now that I've lived there for [y] years. I will lie and tell him that I like being in a place of great freedom and opportunity. It's better to let him think of America as my future home, to let him float past all inconvenient truths. There's no reason to tell him that I will never have enough alphabet to build a room for myself.

The cab will stop at [z] traffic lights, and I'll see change. The city that was once mine is no longer what it was. Every street is altered. I will feel foreign to the city. If my parents do not come to the airport, if they are not alive, I will not know where I am. I might be in the same city, but I will no longer be home. I don't know what I'll be if I don't have a home to go to. I don't know what I'll do if I can't see my experiences reflected in the eyes of someone I love. Home is where rivers die, letter by letter.

I've been working for the *Chicago Tribune* for about five years when it strikes me that I will go home in two months. The ticket has been booked and I'm ready. The phone rings: my mother's lungs have collapsed. She's dead. The funeral is in two days.

My boss reviews the JavaScript code and makes his updates for the day.

The code is in production.

The Zamindar's Watch

When I was little, I'd pretend to be on the phone. Some days the phone was a cornstalk bent around the ear and some days it was a spatula—the instrument didn't matter as much as the news I wished to convey. I'd speak with my friend Sesha, and I'd tell her all the things that couldn't wait until school: "Rani has a new litter," "Dippy is peeing near my house right now," and so on. Occasionally I'd note that my brother was eating like a pig, gobbling more than his fair share of watermelon. And only rarely would I mention something like my father beating my mother; those things were never any fun to talk about.

My father was one of the three barbers in Betalguda. He sat under a banyan tree by the village temple, a dozen feet away from the other two barbers, whom he referred to as "Frogs." They were, he said, old and grubby and shameless enough to night-croak all kinds of things and gobble up his clients. My father dreamed of skinning the two barbers. Such a thing was not permissible, so he sought to defeat them by working longer hours.

An hour before dawn he'd brush his teeth with a neem twig and refill the bottle of eucalyptus oil he used for shaving. He'd make me or my brother, whoever was awake, pack his kit while my mother served him millet and kidney beans. If we pretended to be asleep, he'd stand by our feet and say, "So, when a kid is really sleeping, his or her left leg twitches. Let me see who's sleeping here." My brother and I would promptly move our legs, determined to present ourselves as fully asleep, and my father would bark at whoever caught his fancy that day. It took us a few months to wise up to this trick. He had a lot more like that.

If my mother failed to make his tea with the right amount of sugar, he'd say to her, "You can't do a single thing right." If she was unable to get rid of an oil stain on his shirt, he'd say, "You never do." "You're useless," he'd say to her so often, it became an incantation, a catchphrase. And later I'd find her in the kitchen, fretting over burned curry, repeating to herself, "I'm useless."

But my mother was a genius. She had an extraordinary talent for locating missing objects. All morning she stayed home and cooked and cleaned. In the afternoon, when a neighbor dropped by wailing about a misplaced jhumka, she'd morph into a tracking dog. First she'd find out the weight of the item. Then she'd extract information. A full accounting of all the places you'd been. She'd pace the hut back and forth, stopping briefly to ask questions: dimensions, color, material. She wouldn't rely on memories, where you'd last seen the object and where you thought you'd lost it. "It's the heat. Makes you remember things that never happened," she'd say. And then she'd set off by herself, reconstructing the paths a jhumka might have chosen to wander. "Yes, they have a mind of their own." When she found the object, her smile broke new earth. It was like watching a seed come to life.

We lived in a hut in the fifteenth ward. It would take me ten minutes to walk to school while my brother would get there in eight. There was a stream close by, shallow enough to see the rocks near the shore and dangerously deep in the middle. My brother and I would stop there and throw pebbles into the river and forget our lunch boxes on the shore. At school, children of all ages sat together, and the teacher patrolled the classroom, spending time with each group and shouting at others to keep quiet.

There wasn't much else to do in Betalguda until the summer of 1975, when the Zamindar returned to the village after several years abroad.

Mr. Chandan was in his seventies. His wife had died a long time ago, and his daughter lived in London with her husband, a diplomat. Everybody in the village called Mr. Chandan the Zamindar because his father was once a zamindar and held all the surrounding lands. He had a bungalow for a house and a Premier Padmini car. Not a day went by without all the neighboring kids angling to get in the bungalow and take a deep long look.

In the evenings, the Zamindar sat in his courtyard with a radio, and we'd press our ears against the compound wall to listen to the programming coming out of his Murphy. Every so often a servant would step outside with a stick, and we'd scramble and return home laughing. I'd find my mother shelling peanuts and gabble about the radio, all the things we heard it speak, and she'd sometimes ask, "How much does it weigh?" as if that was the safest way to understand anything.

2

One afternoon my father returned from work and told us that the Zamindar had a telephone installed in his courtyard. He described the telephone as a machine with a cord that coiled like my tresses and spoke into an ear. It was set up on an ivory table with a silk cloth covering the sides, and there was a servant standing near it, tall and buxom, ready to pick up the receiver at any moment and take a message. My father knew this because he'd been summoned for a shave in lieu of the Zamindar's preferred Frog, who'd taken ill.

"So the Zamindar gave me a rupee!" he said, grinning, explaining why he'd come home early. There was no reason to squat under the banyan tree all afternoon and shave a tobacco farmer's armpits for ten paise. He'd made enough money for the whole day.

The Zamindar, he said, wore a watch that glittered like a diamond. It had a yellow lotus for a dial. For the first time in his life, my father said, he couldn't stop staring: "A flower of all things, can you imagine?" He laughed. It was so beautiful he almost gave the Zamindar a nick below the chin. He wondered aloud how much it would cost to buy a watch like that: "Too much, probably." He complimented Mother on the rice she cooked: "Perfectly dry." When I asked him if the telephone looked like the ones we'd seen in touring talkies, he said it looked even better: "Deserves to be seen."

This emboldened us. My brother and I walked the streets, plotting how we could see the telephone without getting into trouble. In the end, there wasn't much of a plan. We—a dozen boys and me, the only adventurous girl—slipped through the front gate.

Coconut trees lined the pathway from the gate to the house. A servant tended to the back garden, and another dozed against a pillar in the courtyard. The telephone was nowhere in sight. The boy leading the battalion forward had a mole on his heel, and I watched it climb and wave. A rooster crowed in the distance, and I wondered as to why it would do so at such an odd time. Sweat pooled down my brother's neck.

We'd barely taken a few steps in when a maid stepped out of the house with the radio. Everyone took cover behind the coconut trees. She set it on a chair and went back inside. We stole forward again. The radio began broadcasting the news, and I heard something about Tashkent. I asked my brother if Tashkent was the name of a politician, but he ignored me. I started calling him Tashkent as a kind of joke, to try to get his attention.

He shushed me, but I kept whispering the name Tashkent anyway. A flesh-colored bug caught my eye and I stopped to inspect it. By the time I looked up, an old man in a yellow khadar had appeared in the courtyard. "Who's there?" he shouted.

Everybody fled past me. I broke into a run and fell, scraping my knees. I called for my brother to wait, but he simply disappeared through the gate. Afterward, for a whole month, I refused to call him anything but Tashkent. This irritated him. He'd argue that it was my fault I got caught, and I'd find it satisfying to say, "Is that so, Tashkent?"

The Zamindar had interesting ears. They were like sorghum fields in the winter, thin patches of hair everywhere. Even when he asked why I'd trespassed on his property, I couldn't stop staring at them. I mumbled something and began to cry.

He asked if I wanted a lemon peel.

I nodded. "Two," I said.

The Zamindar laughed. "Who are you?"

The watch on his wrist glinted in the sun. When the servant, dispatched to get the lemon peel, left his position in the courtyard, I noticed it: an olive-green telephone sitting on an ivory table, just like my father had described. Up until that moment, I hadn't truly understood what a telephone was.

"It's magic, isn't it?" I said, pointing at it.

The Zamindar coughed and spat into a bucket near the chair. "The next time you set foot on my property, I'll break your legs. How's that for magic?"

3

Every time I entered his courtyard, the Zamindar would glance at me and say, "You're here again?" In response, I'd smile sheepishly and linger, and he'd keep listening to the radio. The first couple of times, I sat in the grass and stared at the phone. After that I gained enough confidence to traipse through the garden patting all the bushes.

I decided he was my friend. When I told Mother about my new friend, the Zamindar, she stopped slicing onions and held my shoulders. She made me promise that I wouldn't be alone with a man, no matter how old he was. "Wickedness has no age," she said. "Never trust a man who can't cut his own hair," she added for good measure.

This was typical of her. She was prone to sudden bouts of seriousness; she drew sharp breaths of air and dispatched advice as though she were on her deathbed. All her sayings came in pairs. If you found yourself on the receiving end of one of her precepts, it was only a matter of time before the second came your way. To the neighbor whose son constructed a spindle: "Smartness is relative," and "Don't give a child too many compliments."

To the crow that landed on the windowsill: "No more than a peanut," and "Only hard work can lead you to success."

"The Zamindar's a good fellow!" I told her.

Back then, Sesha and I called everybody a fellow. The kid who got caught wiping his behind at the stream was a "dirty fellow"; the boy who followed Sesha all the way home and asked to touch her chest, a "naughty fellow"; the milkman who wore khakis and rode a bicycle dangling two milk tins, a "milkow"; the postman who got off the midday bus, envelopes tucked underneath his sweaty armpits, a "postow"; the cow that shat on the road to school and refused to budge, a "mooow"; our silly mothers when we asked for ribbon plaits and they braided our hair like the udders of a pig, "sillyows"; and the rice mill owner who, for a little while, cornered Sesha in the dark stretch where cornstalks grew sky-high and repeatedly fondled her until she managed to bite his wrist and run away, a "badow." After that, we stopped. It seemed like the world had enough fellows; there was no point in naming them all.

Evenings when the sun had gone down and dragonflies swarmed around, all the neighboring women sat at their respective doorsteps and gossiped about the Zamindar. When I told them he was my friend, they laughed. One woman said that his family had grabbed enough land that none of their descendants would need to work for a hundred years. Another woman said that if she had that kind of money, she'd wear a new saree every day. The seamstress grew dismayed: If you wore something new every day, would you even notice the pattern work that goes into the zari weave? This would go on until the men returned home, at which point they'd leave mid-discussion and go inside.

Father meanwhile had come to the opinion that a life without a watch wasn't worth living. He said he didn't need an HMT.

Any watch that held his arm and buoyed across time would do. He began working evening hours in a nearby town. He left at dawn and returned home after I slept. Sometimes he missed the last bus and walked four hours to get home after midnight. Late at night, I'd hear his voice sift through my dreams and settle on my chest: "How beautiful is the Zamindar's watch?"

Often, I heard him say to my mother, "I had no idea my arm was this naked." If only his useless wife had brought some money from her family . . .

4

Sesha had "thoughts" about the Zamindar. After the incident with the badow, she had thoughts about everything. The Zamindar, she thought, had fought with his daughter before he came to the village. "He'd rather die than live with her ugly husband."

It wasn't just Sesha. The pandit, stopping for a brief chat on his way to a funeral, said to the schoolteacher that the Zamindar came back because he wanted to die in his own house. At home, the seamstress next door said that the Zamindar was in fact already dying from an obscure disease. On my way to the Zamindar's house, the Marwari around the corner argued with a farmer buying matchsticks at his store: "He should pass here only. Who wants to be buried in a box in some foreign country?"

As soon as I reached the courtyard, I asked the Zamindar, "Are you dying?"

He stopped fiddling with the radio. "Who told you that?"

"The whole village is saying that," I said, saddened at the prospect of losing a friend.

He laughed. "I'm not dying any time soon."

"Thank God," I said, and collapsed on the grass.

The Zamindar smiled. "Are you relieved that you'll still get free lemon peels?"

"I'm relieved that my friend is okay," I said.

He walked toward me and patted my cheek gently like a grandfather.

Perhaps he liked the idea of a child inexplicably devoted to him, or perhaps he simply craved some company. I'd visit, and he'd be listening to the radio; our evenings were no different from before, and yet his demeanor seemed more inviting. Occasionally he'd grunt in response to what he heard on the radio and explain what was happening for my benefit. Every so often he'd ask me a silly question, like what I thought about the Emergency or whether it would rain that night.

Once the Zamindar's face grew soft enough for the servants to gain some courage and start talking among themselves. The cook said that he had been surprised by the softness of the idly at an eatery in the nearby town. He couldn't tell how they had achieved that kind of softness without sacrificing the shape. The gardener asked if the chutney was just as good. In his opinion, the stall by the bus stop had the best chutney and therefore the best idly. The Zamindar spoke suddenly as though he too had been thinking about idly. He said that he had eaten it abroad. The taste was the same; his daughter had made it. She had followed the age-old recipe; she was a good cook. But the way it crumbled in his mouth reminded him of a cake of soap that dissolves into coarse powder as opposed to the melt of freshly churned ghee. He had always thought idly was idly, but he found that the way it broke in his mouth was as elemental to the experience of eating idly as the taste he had come to expect. He had not known or thought about it before. He stopped and fell into a reverie none of us dared to interrupt.

At home, I told my mother that the Zamindar had servants for everything. "He'll shout, 'Leela!' and a maid will clean his earwax."

Mother continued to grate carrots in the lamplight. "What a rich sloth."

I resented the implication that my friend was a sloth. "He's not a sloth, he sits in a chair and thinks deeply," I said.

"What does he think about?" she said.

"Idly."

"Idly? Like breakfast?"

When she said it like that, I no longer felt sure. "Maybe death? I don't know," I said.

"Death?"

"Because he's old?"

Mother stopped grating and looked me in the eye. "Never think about death." She said it as though it was a bad omen to think about death, to invite it into your consciousness, some fundamental principle she believed in.

"Okay, okay," I said.

The follow-up came anyway: "Always choose life."

5

The telephone rang one day when I was in the Zamindar's garden, wrestling with a determined hornet that kept buzzing around my fingers. I'd caught the hornet several times, grazed its wings' pitter-patter, and yet it continued to challenge me. The smell of fried pakora from inside the house prickled my appetite, and I'd started thinking about just letting the hornet win and running home and asking Mother to make me some good hot pakoras.

The servant sprung to pick up the telephone, and the Zamindar leaned forward in anticipation. It sounded like a myna screeching for a partner, only louder and lovelier. Later, as an insurance agent, I'd answer phones for a living, and I'd get sick of the way they bled through my ears, but at the time it felt like there was more music in a single ring than in all the ghazals wheezing on the radio. I ran to pick it up.

The servant got to it first. "Hello, yes, madam, just a minute." The Zamindar approached the phone gingerly and brushed me aside. "Go," he said, gesturing to the garden.

The scent of marigolds strangely made me uneasy as I retraced my steps back to where I'd been a few minutes ago. I stood in the garden watching the Zamindar speak. The hornet returned to circle my feet. I couldn't make out every word. He spoke in small, affectionate cadences, as though his daughter could only understand so much. He smiled briefly, looked at his watch, and said it was beautiful. "You need not have bothered, dear."

The conversation lasted a few minutes. Some of the sentences that came through the air: "Why does an old man like me need a watch?" "Tell him I said hello." "When are you coming home?" "It's the same as before." "Goodbye, dear."

The hornet disappeared and I stood, dear-struck. It had never occurred to me that a father could refer to a daughter in that way. I had always been "girl" or "fool" to my father. I immediately resolved to go home and speak with my dear mother and dear brother and all things dear I found along the way. By the time the Zamindar put down the receiver, I'd already bid adieu to the dear marigolds and had begun walking homeward. The Zamindar shouted, "Hey, schoolgirl." He seemed pleased. "Where are you going?"

I told him I was going home, and he asked where I'd been going before—had I been trying to answer the telephone? "Don't you know you're not supposed to touch other people's things?"

"Can I hold the receiver to my ear—once?"

"No."

I told him I just wanted to hold the phone and say, *Who's there?*

He laughed. "Why?"

"There's no person, only a voice, right? Like a ghost."

"Do you think I just spoke with a ghost?"

I nodded.

The Zamindar became irritated. He said there was nothing special about a telephone. "It's just two people talking."

6

One evening the Zamindar ate Gluco biscuits as he listened to the broadcast. They crunched like sand, and I couldn't look elsewhere; none of us had even tasted one. He held each piece delicately with his index finger and thumb as though the biscuit would crumble if he rested another finger. He brought it to his mouth and took a bite, not eagerly, the way a hungry cat laps up milk, and not sluggishly, like a masticating buffalo, but slowly, gently, as though he had all the time in the world for that biscuit.

The Zamindar caught me staring and sent me home with a pack. "Don't ask for more," he said as he tossed it. The Marwari took notice. He watched from his store as I rationed one piece at a time to my brother as payment for carrying my school bag.

At school, I'd take the pack out of the bag sometimes just to make sure it was still there. Tashkent would mutter, "What a show-off," and draw rabbits in his notebook—he drew whenever he was upset. He was good at drawing, Tashkent, but not very good at understanding that I held all the power; he'd beg me at the river for a biscuit. "Just a little piece," he'd ask.

Days later, when a carton of textbooks arrived from the board of education and the schoolteacher asked if I had said anything to the Zamindar about not having textbooks, I said jokingly, "Of course." He knew that I spent a couple of hours with the Zamindar every day. "Why else would they send us books now?"

The following week, the municipality department took measurements for laying water pipes in our colony and people grew curious. Some would stop me on the street and ask, "What do you two have in common? What do you talk about?" Some, like the Marwari, wanted me to put in a good word. "You don't have to say anything now. If it ever comes up, it'd be nice for the Zamindar to know that I sell Agra matchboxes for the most reasonable prices." When I asked him what I'd get in return, he offered me a matchbox. Sesha and I promptly took the matchbox into the berry patch behind the school and set fire to a clump of dried grass and warmed our hands over the flames.

Later, when I gleefully told my brother that I'd made the Zamindar lay water pipes in our colony, he wouldn't talk to me. He said that I was showboating and that I'd suffer the consequences. That he'd seen everything, that he knew that all I did at the Zamindar's bungalow was sit on the grass and listen. "He's no friend of yours," he said. "You're like a dog to him."

I told Tashkent: First, shut up. Second, he was disrespecting dogs everywhere. Third, he'd picked a convenient time to stop talking to me, just hours after he'd practically begged me for the last Gluco biscuit. He walked away even as I was talking to him, and I screamed, "Cunt," clipping the "t" just like Father did to Mother.

Meanwhile Sesha was convinced that the Zamindar was no longer himself. She felt that the spirit of my dead grandfather had somehow lodged inside the Zamindar and was making him do strange things. She advised that I get everything I wanted from him before the old man came to his senses. "Make him pay," she said, whirling around like a spirit. We pretended that we'd been gifted hundreds of acres, the ones the Zamindar still owned under his name. We roamed the streets holding twigs and ordering armies of ants to water our crops and harvest the produce. "Hey, you, get back in line," Sesha shouted at any solitary ants she saw heading elsewhere.

"No, not like that," I said. "Dear ant, would you please go this way?"

A little niceness goes a long way in ruling ants.

7

Father came back late from town and threw his kit at Mother. He'd been working so hard that when he sat down to eat, his knees quivered for a full minute. "So, this Frog quacks at me when I get down from the bus, and he's so shrill, he says, 'Why are you working in town?' and I say, 'I need to feed my family, why do you care, asshole?' He laughs the weirdest ribbit ever, that motherfucker, then he says, 'I hear you're pimping your daughter.'"

"She's only a child!" my mother said, bringing her hand to her mouth.

He prodded my feet. "You tell me."

My father was a funny man. He would say the most bizarre things and forget them immediately. Once he cracked open the jar of cooking grease and slathered some on our hands and said to my mother that my brother and I were ready to become thieves. That if her father didn't send money like he'd promised, my brother and I would be sent on a nighttime adventure. When I asked him the next morning if he'd really make us thieves, he told us to stop playing games. He looked at our hands and yelled, "Why are they so oily?"

Since the Zamindar adored me and offered me gifts, my father said that the next time I went there I should ask for his watch.

I told my father that I couldn't ask the Zamindar for anything, Tashkent could testify to that, couldn't he? I could hardly bring myself to ask him for another pack of biscuits, least of all his watch.

"Then don't ask him. Bring it," he said.

8

The radio fizzled and died. No matter how many times the Zamindar pried it open and put it back together, it wouldn't talk. The sun had gone down, and there was an orange blaze etched into the sky. Wind howled.

"What's the time on your watch?" I said.

The Zamindar smiled. "Why do you care about time?"

It was true, I had no use for time. Every morning I woke up around dawn, sometimes because of the light, sometimes because of the rooster on the next street or the noises in the kitchen; mostly because I'd slept enough. We went to school after the morning bus came from town. It came around nine in the morning and let out a jet of air so loud that Tashkent used to say, "The bus has already farted, you haven't gotten ready yet?" When the sun burned directly above our heads, we took our lunch boxes and sat under the peepal tree. A couple of hours after lunch, when he could no longer stay awake, the school-teacher let us go. We went to bed a couple of hours after dusk. That was just how things were. It wasn't until much later, when I worked in the insurance office six days a week, twelve hours a day, that I knew what a luxury it was.

"What's the time on the watch?" I said.

"Why?"

"Does the dial glow in the dark?"

He said nothing, chin curled up like a dormouse.

"Can I see it?" I asked.

He held up his hand, and the yellow lotus came into view. Pretty.

"Can I hold it? Please?" I asked, extending my hand.

"Enough, go home," he said, rising from his chair.

9

The next morning the police took my father away. One of the Frogs had woken up at midnight to take a leak and seen him scampering toward the patch of marshland called Payela, where they burned all the hair that had been cut every year. This, the constable said, corresponded with the time the Zamindar noticed his watch went missing.

The constable had an interesting nose. It was long and thin and speckled. He pulled on it and said "okay" every time he spoke, as though both disgusted and satisfied by what he saw. Chewing betel nuts, he walked around the kitchen turning vessels upside down. "Okay. Where did he hide it?"

"It's not here. He didn't steal it," Mother said.

"Okay. Sure, I believe you," he said with a snicker.

"My husband is not a thief."

"Okay. Then where was he last night around midnight?"

Mother fell silent. "He was working in the town!" I said.

The constable turned toward me. They knew, he said, of my interest in the Zamindar's watch. "You must have stolen it, not your father," he said, and laughed at his own joke, the nose going up and down like a water pump.

My brother said, "Please, sir, my sister is innocent."

"Okay. Then you come with me," he said, and dragged Tashkent into his jeep.

At the police station Tashkent was kept in a cell and hung upside down from the ceiling with a thick rope that cut into his ankles. He swung a little, arms reaching for the floor. He didn't seem to register our presence.

The police said that Tashkent would be sent home as soon as my father talked. Or as soon as we produced the watch. "Make my life easy, okay?"

10

Even from a distance the Payela looked like an armpit. There was a depression, a hollow connecting the grassy part of the land with the marshy areas. The hollow stayed wet most of the year except in summer, when algae took over. When a strong breeze hit, tufts of hair rolled in the air. Mother ripped the edge of her pallu in two and gave me a piece. We held the cloth around our noses, stepping on small mounds of thick black hair.

"Do you think you can find it?" I asked, picking hair off my arms and chin.

"Shh." Mother closed her eyes.

The sun brightened everything, blades of grass now a mosaic of cut mirrors. If Father hadn't come until after midnight, if he'd indeed stolen the watch, if what people were saying was true, this was our best chance of getting Tashkent back. I closed my eyes, imitating her, willing myself to hear it, smell it, find it.

"Did it look heavy?" Mother asked.

"Kind of." I'd already told her everything I knew about the watch: the shape, the size, the dial, the yellow lotus.

"Either there is a mountain or there isn't." She pushed down my shoulders. "Never find yourself in the middle of a gray area." She seemed exasperated. I wondered if she was talking about my father.

Sifting through a putrid mound of hair, we discovered three dried orange peels, a twig, two plastic covers, broken pencil bits, the rotting carcass of a field rat, and excreta of some kind. At the bottom, ink bugs dotted the floor. "Watch out. They'll stick to your feet," she said.

I lost track of the number of mounds in front of us. "What's the plan?"

"Keep your eyes on the ground."

Sweat lined her forehead and she wiped it with the cloth she'd been holding to her nose. We went from one corner to another, one arm to the nose and one arm on the ground, working mound after mound. Each time the results were the same or nearly the same combination of animal remains and garbage.

The sun moved above our heads. My back began to hurt.

"I thought you'd have found it by now," I said.

"I'm useless," she said, knees buckling to the ground.

"You're not useless. You're a genius," I said, suddenly feeling stupid.

She laughed bitterly. "Is that what you tell your friends? I'm not a genius. I'm just a pebble on the ground."

"Do you think he's still hanging upside down?"

She burst into tears and moved frantically, arms foraging through the mounds wildly like monkeys in front of the temple. Again, I'd said the wrong thing. I crouched down. A couple of ink bugs on top of a small mound. I called out to them: "Dear ink bugs, where are you going?"

Mother turned around. "What did you say?"

I pointed at the ink bugs.

"Their blood is blue," she said, her face now a sapling. She began combing through the patch, looking for smudges of blue, for hair that had been stepped on.

Soon we had a path. A speck of color here and there, connecting one mound to another. Every time we found hair with bluish discoloration, Mother exhaled loudly. The trail stopped at an ordinary mound of hair. It smelled like urine.

Abandoning the nose cloths, Mother and I waded through the hair: lice, rotten banana, insect larvae, empty can of pesticide, hair. Just hair. At the very bottom, a pencil case.

"I knew you were a genius," I said, jumping up and down.

She opened the case. Out came a lump of hair.

II

When he finally came home, Tashkent would not speak. He had a big gash on his thigh and his knuckles were bandaged. Judging by the way he screamed when Mother cleaned his wound, his tongue was fine. But the only way he would communicate was with a pencil. Mother would give him a piece of paper and ask how many roti he wanted, and he'd draw a plate with two roti. When I asked him what happened at the police station, he scraped furiously until the paper tore. A week later he jumped in the stream where we used to fling stones. When they retrieved his body, his face looked calm. After that I refused to let myself say his name. I decided he was forever Tashkent.

My father came home after six months. He had swollen eyes, a large beard, and a pronounced limp. He said that the watch had been found in a small crack in the Zamindar's bed. He looked at Mother and said, "So what happens to our son now?"

We left Betalguda and moved to a town in the south where nobody knew us. It rained a lot there. The streets were always awash with rainwater, and there were open manholes. I learned to look down when walking. Groups of boys often splashed each other and raced paper boats. When Mother and I made our way to a nearby store, I'd find black sludge under my nails. And I'd catch Mother standing still, watching the boys race past us.

Mother began working as an ayah. She mopped offices and cleaned toilets and paid for my education. She'd come home every evening and complain of heel pain. My father mellowed out a bit, but not a whole lot. He still swore and ate brinjals like they were going extinct. He still woke up at dawn and cut people's hair. But at midnight, he broke into cold fits and pressed Mother's feet until she woke up and told him to sleep. This lasted a few months.

Then my father left. Nobody could find him. Not even my mother.

12

The last time I saw the Zamindar, we'd begun packing to leave. I'd said goodbye to Sesha and was walking homeward when his car sped past me. Laughing in the car with him: his daughter and son-in-law and grandson. It was rumored that they'd convinced the Zamindar to sell his properties and transfer all his money into an investment fund that could be managed from abroad. The Zamindar sat in the front seat along with the driver. The rest of the family sat in the back. He seemed content. I wished he'd get cancer.

Twenty years later, as luck would have it, it was my mother who contracted cancer. Her gallbladder was gone. The hospital had her connected to several machines that buzzed and chimed. I'd feed her the idly I brought from home, and she'd talk more than she ate. She remembered things I'd long forgotten: the way my father had tricked me and Tashkent into revealing we were awake, the time she found the seamstress's earring, how oranges tasted back in Betalguda. She wanted to chat all the time. "What else is new?" she'd ask at lunch, even though we'd spoken at breakfast. I'd read her the newspaper. "What are these economic reforms?" she'd say, and I'd shrug. I'd tell her about my job. About the insurance policies I renewed. About the calls I fielded. About the claims questions I answered a thousand times. By then, I had married a man who was every bit as mean and as funny as my father. I'd wake up every morning and feel a weight on my chest, a boulder under my rib cage, straining my legs, pulling me down to the ground, and I'd lie on my side on the floor listening to the daily growl of vehicles on the street.

Mother would look at me and shake her head when I entered

her room. When I asked her what was wrong, she would say, "What else is new?"

She said this every morning, and then she died.

A week before she died, she rested her palm on my hand and said that she wanted to tell me something. She ran her fingers over my knuckles and told me that all her life she'd enjoyed finding things that had gone missing, because it felt good to be in control of her life for those few hours. "Don't do that to yourself," she said. "It's not worth it, kanna."

She described her marriage with my father as a "darbar," an emperor's court. Sometimes you were an object of ridicule, sometimes you were granted kindness, sometimes you were a witness, often you were a worker, a maid, or a cunt, but you were always watching him watch.

Days later, when I told her about a man who had his wife dashed by a truck so he could get the insurance payout, she coughed and exclaimed that throughout history people have always been animals. I stared at her pale and crusty feet; I could feel the proverbs coming my way. "Never let a man insure you," she said. I laughed and waited for the follow-up, the second instruction, but it would never arrive. Her mouth stayed open.

She was now earth. Lost somewhere in her trachea: a phrase that would tell me how to live this life. It was meant for me, this message. I told myself that nothing was lost forever. Sooner or later, I'd hear it. I imagined her words reaching me through someone else's mouth. A song humming in my ears. A voice in the night. Every time the phone rang, I picked up and listened for a whisper. Someone always said hello.

The Sea

Since her body was lost at sea, there was no Janazah.

An assortment of people visited Rafi's house and spoke in hushed voices: friends going as far back as high school, relatives who happened to be in the city, fellow teachers from Bhimili Government School, acquaintances from the masjid he rarely visited, the Vizag chapter of Marxist scholars and thinkers. Rafi would never have put them all in the same room.

Be strong, they said, taking turns. They held him by the shoulder and remembered things about Nur. She'd asked after someone's ailing parents, she'd sent sweets to an orphanage, she'd taken someone's matrimonial pictures, she'd done this, she'd done that. Rafi waited for them to stop talking about Nur so *he* could talk to her.

Look how many people came, Rafi wanted to tell Nur. She'd have been excited to meet them; she loved hosting people. Between the two of them, he was the loner and she was the glue. It wasn't supposed to have been this way. A boat ride to the nearby island, the same old tourist destination in the Bay of Bengal; lunch with her old friend and some sightseeing; back home in time for dinner—that was what he'd expected. When the boat capsized and the news channel declared twelve people dead, he thought she'd call him and tell him about the catastrophe she'd witnessed. Instead, he'd chased after divers and police to search for her dead body.

Someone handed him a phone. Nur's mother was calling from London, where she lived with Nur's sister and family. He couldn't hear any words at first, just her crying. It bothered Nur's mother that they couldn't have the Janazah, that Allah hadn't even allowed them the concession of holding Nur's body and draping her in a white linen cloth.

Rafi hung up when she started crying again. Then he asked everybody to leave.

From that moment on, Rafi lived by an abiding principle. He'd try not to think about Nur. Every time she came to mind, he'd shut down the past, he'd say no to the memory. This principle, he felt, was important. Otherwise, how was he to survive?

Day 14

Rafi walked toward the beach. He stopped for a cow moseying across the road and saw the aquarium shop across the way. He remembered Nur thrusting goggles in his face, taunting him to dunk his head inside an aquarium and look at the goldfish. Why don't you test it, Master ji—that's what she called him, Master ji, but only when she found him cute. As though the thing she liked best about him and his books was that he remained inaccessible to everyone but her, and when she wasn't frustrated with him, she'd plant a kiss on his forehead and say that he was an *item* that belonged in the museum, and he'd shake his head thinking, *My stupid woman,* you *belong in a museum—no.*

He'd nearly reached the turn that led toward the beach when he heard a shout, the voice clearly Chacha's. Rafi took a few steps back to Malik Chacha's kirana and faced him. Malik Chacha in his white kurta, drinking tea. Chacha, that was what Nur called him. Technically he wasn't his chacha, but it stuck.

Have you heard anything from the police? Chacha asked.

No, Rafi said. He'd requested that the police inspector approve another search, and the inspector had said, What do you want us to do, search the entire sea for a dead Muslim woman?

Chacha took another sip. Kareem told me two bodies washed to the shore, near the port.

Old news, Chacha, Rafi said. I saw them, a couple of tourists, thighs chewed, eyes gone.

Chacha closed his eyes. Inna lillahi wa inna ilayhi raji'un.

A group of schoolkids walked past them, past Chacha's kirana, and streamed into the Hindu-owned store next door. Rafi watched as one of them angled after a fifty-paise toffee. Nur loved that toffee. She was so spoiled; she'd had unlimited access to Chacha's store and took chocolates, soaps, hair creams, whatever she wanted. She'd wanted the best of everything the world could offer—TV, AC, car, house. He was always surprised at the intensity of her desires, had even mocked her by saying she was like a child at a fair—*no*.

Two weeks already, Chacha said, bringing the tea glass to his mouth and putting it away.

Rafi stayed silent.

Chacha sighed. Master ji this, Master ji that, she used to call you—

Rafi shrugged. How's business?

Beta, Chacha said, you have to be strong—

Chacha's assistant arrived holding a ledger and a cell phone. Chacha took the phone and began to talk. Rafi drifted away.

Day 23

Chalk dust flitted in the air. The parallelogram problem Rafi drew on the chalkboard stymied his students. He walked around, watching them scribble random numbers in the margins of their notebooks, thankful for the structure teaching brought to his life.

He looked at his best student, a Dalit boy who walked three miles to get to school. The boy, he picked up from a cursory glance, had made a rudimentary error in the first angle calculation that broke his subsequent calculations. Try for two more minutes, he said to the class, to give the boy more time.

He'd told Nur about the boy, and she'd gotten jealous, that even after coming home all he talked about were his students—*no*.

Students of all grades gave him no trouble in class; they were respectful and sincere. The whole town too. The YMCA manager opened his office door as soon as he saw Rafi lingering outside and gave him a special discount for the swimming lessons he sought. In the local bookstore, the owner had whispered in his ear that he could take any book home and return it after he'd read it. At the market, vendors snuck in a couple extra tomatoes and limes along with the other groceries he'd bought. At the cinema, his colleagues bought him popcorn. On the bus, the conductor forgot to ticket him. At home, the neighbors sent their boy to give him chai. In the bathroom, the tap that leaked refused to leak.

Day 38

Rafi's eyes fell on the mint plant, pale and dying. The only plant she could keep alive, he'd always teased her about it. He bent over it, inspecting. He took a broken twig and traced circles in the soil. It wasn't beyond hope. He grabbed a cup of water and emptied it into the pot.

He'd stripped the living room of all their furniture; there was just one last chair left. He hadn't managed to sell it yet; he'd ask his colleagues if they'd take it off his hands.

Rafi went to his study. The sixth-grade question paper he'd put off writing, he needed to finish it. He sat at his desk and stretched out his legs. The question paper, he said to himself, opening the math textbook. A slip fell from the book and he bent to retrieve it, a receipt from the local bookstore. Then he saw it, lying under the desk, her blue sock. How it had ended up there and why there was only one, he had no idea; she never entered his study except to clean or give him chai, and she always left with a reminder that he should rinse the cup right away before putting it in the sink and he'd argue that he didn't want to break away from whatever he was working on—*no*.

Picking it up, he smelled. Nothing, there was no smell. He unlocked the bedroom door and ignored the dust accumulating on top of the pile of boxes pushed against the wall. He opened one and shoved the sock inside. Locking the door, he felt the dust on his fingertips; he washed his hands in the common bathroom and returned to the study.

The new cot in his study beckoned him. He thought of lying down for a little bit, but the question paper deadline flashed in his mind. He hunkered down and looked through some of the geometry exercises for good questions. *If two lines are cut by a transversal and the alternate interior angles are congruent, are the lines parallel?*

Day 65

BHIMILI GOVERNMENT SCHOOL, the new signboard said. Rafi watched as the headmaster surveyed it. He remembered standing in the same spot eight years ago. The school was on a cliff and he'd never seen the sea before, and the principal had introduced him to the other teachers and insisted that he walk beyond the classrooms and look at the sea. He walked past empty classrooms and around a clutter of coconut trees and found himself face-to-face with it. Spanning as far as he could see, the big blue monster clawed at the coast. Waves crashed inward, littering the shore with seaweed. It seemed passionate: here was something that fell in love with the sky and shaped itself in the image of its lover. He imagined being caught in the swirls of something so vast, and a desire to maintain a respectful distance sprung inside him.

Can't believe it's been eight years, Rafi said.

Don't take this the wrong way, the principal said. You're under forty. You should get married again. Life has to go on.

He heard this from the police when he'd asked them if anything had been found: Go marry again, isn't it normal for you guys to have more than one wife?

Maybe the principal hadn't meant it in that way; he was a decent upper-caste Hindu. But even the principal, he remembered, had been a little wary of him initially, looking at him with a pinch of fear even though he'd never grown a beard or done namaz at school. It was as if contained within his name, within his hands and legs and chest and face and hair, there was a strange terror that could unleash at any minute.

Once the principal learned he was practically secular, the fear went away.

I have to go, sir, Rafi said, not wanting to hear any more talk of wives.

Day 106

Rafi flailed in the YMCA pool reaching for the sidebar. *Nur,* he'd heard someone say. Sounded like a man's voice, but it could have been a child's too. Like it was summoning her. He held the sidebar and observed people in the pool. They were busy splashing. Was it an echo the chlorinated water uttered as her name?

The instructor saw him and swam over. What is it? he asked.

Nothing, Rafi said. He took deep breaths.

It's just water, you know how to swim. Don't be scared, let the water carry you, the instructor said, smiling. Float, relax.

Rafi tried to relax, to stop thinking. The problem was his mind. It was too active. He needed to push away any thoughts about how it would feel to swim in the sea, and maybe then he'd actually master swimming. He fell back into the pool. Conscious breathing. He began to relax, and the instructor moved away.

Rafi swam a couple of laps and stopped and felt the waves travel outward and return. Floating in the swimming pool. *What a waste of time, could have read Gramsci instead,* his earlier self would have said, the self that told Nur that capitalism was making everyone a consumerist and that there was no need to get six bottles of artificial mango juice when they knew she'd get sick of it after two, and she'd cried in her bedroom saying all he saw her as was a pretty woman who couldn't think—*no*.

Water dripped off his arms as he stepped out of the swimming pool. In the men's room, he rubbed his limbs dry.

Day 267

At a colleague's wedding, Rafi laughed when someone joked about marriage being the only factory in town, that sooner than later you'd have to eat the salt that came out of it. He laughed freely. He remembered the way he'd been set up.

It's high time, the people around him had said.

If you don't marry now, you'll be a shriveled mushroom no one wants, they said.

She's perfect, they pitched.

He secretly made plans to catch a glimpse of her. He saw her on the city bus sitting next to a friend. She'd raised her dainty eyes and laughed at something her friend said. The laugh, what a laugh, lighting up her cheeks, coloring her nose pink, like a princess who could only bring uncontrollable joy.

And just like that, he'd been married. The initial days were all haze and light. He ran home from school for lunch and struggled to eat anything other than her face. He waited until the end of his lunch hour to stuff his mouth with the nihari she'd made before tearing himself away. He peeked at his watch multiple times during his lessons and abandoned his class as soon as the bell rang. The next few hours, until they slept exhausted, were pure torture. He didn't know how to guide it in, and she was too small, but they somehow managed. Bodies intermingled, they uncovered the sweet rim of past lives. She slept on his chest breathing ancient joy.

Soon enough, he'd walk home and find her watching TV. She'd insist on finishing a serial she was watching while they ate. Gone were the extended hugs; no more dashing to the door. They talked about the things that happened while the other was away. Deep conversations were over. Or rather, what he thought of their deep conversation was only the strange fullness of attention and desire for someone new and intimate in your life.

He was careful at school; he knew not to reveal that he helped cook. He understood the ways in which women were shackled, wanted her to be free to do her own thing, but he couldn't tell what that was. She never read a book. And when he sat with a book, desiring nothing more than a quiet evening, she hovered around him, wanting them to go out: Ooh, let's walk by the beach and get some salted peas and look at shoes—and maybe ask if they had the model with blue beads that she'd once considered buying.

Evenings, he'd watch her step into the wet of the sand vacated by the sea. Like a child, she'd run back to him before the wave rushed for her feet.

He wanted all the other memories to visit. *Come,* he said to them.

No, they said.

Day 278

Rafi's arms began to feel sore. He'd swum back and forth for a long time. The instructor came to him and said, Doing good, which pleased him. He wondered if that was how his students felt when he commended them. In the water, now, he felt fine. He felt good.

Exhausted from the swim, but still in a fugue state an hour after he reached home, Rafi got on the internet. He'd tried reading Herbert Marcuse, but his attention span was not the same. The internet was a strange place, a time warp. He found himself reading random things, things he didn't need to know. He'd never been outside India, but he looked at an article that popped up on *Jacobin,* on how the housing crisis had developed in San Francisco. He walked through the maps that were linked to in the article, taking endless detours into alleys with exercise studios and gift stores and organic cafés, all of which were useless to him, and yet he kept clicking to see if he'd find something that would hold his interest. The internet was an exercise in futility, a torchlight to the insignificance of his life. And yet, once in a while, he'd stumble on to something that could keep him going for hours. That's how he'd found out that jellyfish outdated dinosaurs. That dolphins can sleep with only half their brain and with one eye open. And that bit about sea sponges—he couldn't believe that they have no head, mouth, eyes, bones, heart, lungs, or brain, and yet, they are alive! Like a bureaucrat transferred to a different department, his interest in Marxist politics and culture was transferred to the sea. Looking up facts about the sea and the creatures it hid, he fell asleep at his desk.

He dreamed he was a dog prowling behind a gate, leaping back and forth, feet walloping the ground, eyeing people outside. Street cleaners collected trash on the road and stopped to gossip. Morning joggers greeted old women strolling down the street, and suddenly he felt the need to bark. He let one go, but he couldn't hear it. He tried again, but it was distant and inaudible, like a bark underwater. Rafi woke up, and the dream slipped out of his mind, but on the desk, it was obvious that he'd drooled like a dog.

He touched his cheek and felt hard outlines from the wood.

Day 389

Mist on Rafi's nose. Early-morning light dipped from the sky into the sea, a dull, pulsing color that ran furious. Sand particles on his cheek, the wind against him. As the lash of the sea grew louder, his heart began to thump. Waves tore at his knees. The first gush of water went into his nose. He shook it off and dove inside.

A silence came over him, an absolute peace. He touched his goggles to make sure the straps were all right. The silence in the sea grew to a point where he could hear music again, Nur urging him to dance with her instead of reading a history book, Nur pleading with him to go to London on vacation, Nur suggesting that they immigrate to a country where things were better, Nur requesting that he rinse his cup of chai before putting it in the sink, Nur demanding that he not think about school after coming home, Nur asking him to come out of his study and spend time with her. And all he ever said was no.

But the thing about the sea was that it was old and vast: 90 percent of all living organisms existed in the abyss, coral reefs had sparkled below the surface for centuries, and there was a time in the past when it draped the entire earth.

All he had to do was hold her.

Best Possible Experience

From the beginning, Mr. Lourenco stood by his promises. If he told Alex that he would pick him up from school, he most certainly would.

Alex stood outside St. Stephen's Convent in Goa and waited for his father while some of his classmates summoned their chauffeurs. Vehicles of all kinds racketed their way to the children. Car kids sniggered at scooter kids. Scooter kids sniggered at bicycle kids. Bicycle kids sniggered at walking kids. They all turned to Alex. Clouds grumbled and he gazed upward. He decided to look at the overcast sky until all the judgmental kids were gone.

Then a tourist bus stormed into the schoolyard, dwarfing all the other vehicles. Mr. Lourenco's head popped out the driver's window. He honked a Konkani song, or some distant cousin of it. He stuck out a hand and waved. Alex boarded the bus, leaving the others thunderstruck.

The bus had a lot of people on board, both tourists and locals. Some of the locals were taking their visiting relatives to the basilica. Some were Russian backpackers. There were four Indian families from Bombay. An elderly French couple sat in the first row, contemplating what the historical significance of this school might be that it merited a stop on the tour.

Mr. Lourenco introduced Alex to the bunch and told them his son was in third grade. He grabbed a child seat and had Alex sit next to the French couple. The old lady searched her purse and gave him a chocolate bar. Alex sought Mr. Lourenco's eye, and once the approval came, he bit into it with utter abandon.

The bus honked past everything on the road and stopped at the Magnificent Rock.

Ladies and gentlemen, here is the Magnificent Rock. Mr. Lourenco pointed out the window. An oval-shaped rock the size of a three-story building lay drenched in rain. Tourists scrambled to the right side of the bus and collectively gasped.

Mr. Lourenco smiled at the delight in their faces, the wondrous delight of seeing in full rainy glory the aforementioned rock. Magnificent indeed, a backpacker agreed. Pomp sei la fantastique, said the old lady. She had actually said something else, but that was what Alex heard.

The locals were unimpressed. The big, bearded Goan wanted Mr. Lourenco to continue on to the next point, the Unflowering Gardens, where his cousin owned a gift shop. Some advocated for the basilica. One local, a bald man with thick glasses, turned on a handheld radio and listened to folk songs while he asked Mr. Lourenco to hurry up and drop him at the library. An electricity department clerk, a regular on the bus, downed the Magnificent Rock and upped the Over Bridge, which was a short walk from his office. Another local, a burly cop, insisted they go straight to the police station.

Anger, usually a foreign emotion, invaded Alex. What business did they have on this tourist bus? They paid the fare, he knew. Except, of course, the cop, who spread his legs across two seats, who clearly felt that they should be basking in the privilege of transporting him. These people irritated him; their behavior was an insult to Mr. Lourenco. Did they realize how tactfully Mr. Lourenco had avoided Aldona Road, which was often the quickest way to get to the Magnificent Rock but prone to flooding at the slightest bit of rain? Had they paid any attention to how swiftly Mr. Lourenco had overtaken a tractor that had been in the way so that they could have a few extra seconds to fully appreciate the rock? Had they noticed how Mr. Lourenco, sensing their eagerness, had limited his speech to *Ladies and gentlemen, here is the Magnificent Rock,* but operatically stressed *the Magnificent Rock* to stir their hearts and put them in the best possible state to have the best possible experience so that they could sleep that night with satisfaction, the kind of satisfaction that comes from having gained a spectacular memory, and attain, as a result, the best possible sleep of their lives? No, they knew nothing. They had all scrambled to look at the Magnificent Rock, oblivious, and now they were demanding Mr. Lourenco drive elsewhere, ruining the experience for others.

Mr. Lourenco didn't seem angry. On the contrary, he laughed. Of course, we'll go wherever you want, he humored them. Do you know the secret history of this lamp?

He pointed to a bronze lamp by the side of the road. They shook their heads, and he spoke as he drove:

It isn't just any lamp. Queen Catarina of Portugal sent boatloads of órfãs do rei, orphan girls, to the Portuguese state of India, exclusively for the benefit of Portuguese soldiers. These orphan girls, they were white, Catholic, and exceedingly pretty. Unfortunately for the Portuguese, more órfãs do rei arrived than eligible men, and the establishment didn't want them mixing with Indians. So what they did was they gave some of them postal responsibilities. A certain Lisa was among these girls. Said to be the prettiest of all, she didn't have a man to marry.

After a brief courtship, she accepted a marriage proposal from an Indian working at the post office. The establishment found out and chained the poor thing to that lamp as an example for the others. Over time, things became more relaxed, and some órfãs do rei married Indians and led happy lives. But think about Lisa. Tied to that lamp, she languished.

They all thought about Lisa. The locals fell silent, imagining how they might have saved Lisa and married her. The French couple acknowledged the weight of imperialism with long, contemplative faces. Alex had tears in his eyes; he'd never heard about Lisa before. What a wonderful history lesson Mr. Lourenco had imparted.

Later, at home, he'd find out the truth when Mr. Lourenco asked him why he was sad, and he told Mr. Lourenco that he was feeling sorry for Lisa, and Mr. Lourenco laughed and told him Lisa had never existed. And it would be insightful for him to hear that Mr. Lourenco had made up Lisa to prevent the locals from spoiling the best possible experience for the tourists. But the story wasn't true, Alex would say. And Mr. Lourenco would explain órfãs do rei did exist, his own grandmother was probably one, and history books said that some órfãs do rei married locals, and so wasn't it possible that such a Lisa could have existed? Wouldn't the establishment have been furious? Wasn't it possible that a Lisa-like figure could have been punished in that way? Alex would find himself nodding, and Mr. Lourenco would go on to impart a wonderful lesson about delivering the best possible experience.

These tourists, he'd tell Alex, need to escape the monotony of their lives. What was most enjoyable to them was learning about history, the thrill of imagining other lives. It was his duty, as a bus driver of Tourist Bus Company, as a person of taste, to give these people exactly what they needed. If showing them some old building and telling them it was the first one the Portuguese had built made them construct in their heads an image of white men on horses flogging natives and supervising the construction, wouldn't they lose themselves for a moment in that image? Wouldn't they be satisfied with the feeling of standing amid history, of being in the exact place where these white men had once stood? If going back in time and experiencing an aha moment via a Portuguese state building made their experience richer, there was no harm in that building being this one. They, Alex and Mr. Lourenco, were doing the noble work of uplifting spirits.

Alex received so many such lessons over the years, and they all made him proud of Mr. Lourenco. They were not like regular people—Mr. Lourenco had taught him to be different. He could ask Mr. Lourenco anything and he'd get nothing but the truth. More than father and son, he felt they were like old friends, ready to die for each other. Mr. Lourenco would sometimes get the bus out at night, and they'd go to a movie. They'd liked *Great Expectations* so much they agreed Alex would call his father Mr. Lourenco, like a certain Pip in the movie, who acquired culture by politely addressing older men as Mr. It adds culture, Mr. Lourenco had said. Eating beef didn't make them sophisticated; seafood did, and so they ate oysters and sea bass for a while, and when they found it too expensive, they stuck to vegetarianism.

There were other ideas, initially thought to bring culture but soon discarded. Among those: starting a radio station, cross-country running, smoking Cuban cigars, record mixing, candlepin bowling. Unfortunately, the general public appropriated some of those ideas themselves and sucked the joy out of them. Except for airports and the business of flying. Even in later years, when people from their neighborhood flew all over the world and complained about the experience, Mr. Lourenco thought it extraordinary. According to Mr. Lourenco, there was something to be said about the feeling of soaring over tractors and auto-rickshaws, cars and buildings and cities, all of humanity.

And so, beginning that summer, the Tourist Bus Company's tourist bus added an unscheduled stop to its service: the airport. Construction had just begun on the terminal, but already a cargo flight landed every Tuesday. The airstrip that initially had been built by the Portuguese state was torn down and relaid. Occasionally some military planes landed. Every day Mr. Lourenco stopped the bus at the entrance and estimated progress. If there was a military flight on the horizon, the bus would move only after it had come to a stop. On the rare occasion they saw a takeoff, Mr. Lourenco had Alex distribute sweets. When the locals nagged at him to keep driving, Mr. Lourenco turned around and launched into a story. Did you know, he'd say, there were once flights from here to Mozambique?

When Mr. Lourenco was fired from the Tourist Bus Company, he brooded for six hours and promised Alex that he would get the job back. He should never have been fired; he'd asked for four days off and taken Alex to Bombay for plane-watching, and his replacement had secured his job on a permanent basis by telling the boss all kinds of things about him: Mr. Lourenco often took the bus out at night (true), he made stops out of route and wasted fuel for airport trips (true), and he'd begun to teach his twelve-year-old son how to drive the bus (also true). But in what context were these accusations being made? Mr. Lourenco questioned the motives behind the revelations.

Zero moral values, Mr. Lourenco said to Alex. A tattler does not care about anybody's benefit but his own. Forget about giving the best possible experience—employing such a driver would bankrupt the Tourist Bus Company.

Alex was sure that this cheating scum of a driver must be very similar to the driver they'd endured in Bombay, and therefore they needn't worry—the guy wouldn't last, and the owner would come begging for Mr. Lourenco's return.

In Bombay, Mr. Lourenco and Alex had ridden a tourist bus while they were exploring the city. But they'd been dismayed to find that tourist buses had a guide who did all the talking. The driver and guide were two different people, and this caused all sorts of problems—the driver's actions and the guide's comments were not synchronized.

When the driver approached Victoria Terminus, the guide spoke about the railway network in Bombay, mere factual information—when, what, where. He hadn't even pointed to the Victoria Terminus yet when the traffic light turned green and the driver took a right, and the guide hastily gestured at the terminus and the passengers had to spin their necks so sharply they'd very likely end up suffering from neck pain later that night, which would lead to the worst possible sleep of their lives. Mr. Lourenco hoped such a system would never come to Goa. The whole thing was impersonal and, to his mind, signaled the collapse of public morality. He reiterated his cherished lesson on the art of service. Their work, Mr. Lourenco said, was vital. There were too many sad people traipsing around their lives who needed moments of solace and communion with the wider world, and it was their duty to provide that space for them, but right then Mr. Lourenco learned that the tourist bus wouldn't even go to the Bombay airport and that the driver wouldn't take them. They got off at the zoo instead and saw all kinds of creatures. Alex had never seen so many birds in one place. He assumed Mr. Lourenco would be all over them for their ability to fly, but he seemed more smitten with the Bengal tiger. They paid one rupee for a photograph in front of the tiger exhibit. Then they wolfed down vada pav at the zoo canteen and caught a city bus to the airport.

At the airport, Mr. Lourenco bounced on his toes, and Alex counted four planes in ten minutes. The security officer wouldn't let them inside the terminal without a ticket. Mr. Lourenco pleaded with the guard to no effect. After an hour of hard thinking, they went back and bribed the guard with five rupees so that Alex could go inside for a few minutes; they figured he was small enough to avoid scrutiny. Alex came back with precise descriptions of what he saw. There were multiple counters, each three feet apart, each for a different airline. They hadn't known there were multiple airlines. Mr. Lourenco had assumed that the central government controlled all aviation. Alex relayed many equally surprising details to him, but of all the things that surprised Mr. Lourenco, the most surprising was that passengers had to wait in a queue to drop their bags—who knew!

When they returned to Goa, Mr. Lourenco's boss gave him the news. The devastation Mr. Lourenco felt was not the slightest, Alex had never seen him so quiet.

But Mr. Lourenco soon came up with a plan. He took Alex with him to meet the owner of the Tourist Bus Company. The owner, a six-foot-tall Punjabi ex-wrestler, had black-and-white wrestling photos framed in his office. The moment he saw Alex, he accused Mr. Lourenco of bringing the boy to guilt him into giving his job back. He also accused Mr. Lourenco of doing the same thing to get a raise after Alex's mother had died.

Mr. Lourenco could not have the job back. The new driver, he ranted, made more trips than Mr. Lourenco did with the same amount of fuel. Mr. Lourenco folded his arms and agreed and apologized until the owner paused to breathe. Then he launched into a defense of his art. Sure, the new guy saved money, but in the long run, business would fall. The new guy didn't know much history, so the owner would have to hire a guide to do all the talking, which was exactly what tourist companies were doing in Bombay, Mr. Lourenco noted. But he could do both jobs for one salary. The owner sighed and said he'd think about it. When they stepped out of the office, Mr. Lourenco whooped with joy.

Alex was in high school the next time Mr. Lourenco promised him something. Alex had by then come around to the idea of becoming a pilot—the best possible profession, according to Mr. Lourenco. But he knew they couldn't afford flight school. And yet Mr. Lourenco kept insisting that he would make it happen.

There were several things about Mr. Lourenco that were beginning to exasperate Alex. Years of street food had given Mr. Lourenco a large potbelly, and when Alex told him to exercise, all he did was walk around the block for five minutes and then help himself, later that night, to an extra serving of kheer at Qureshi's Café, their regular haunt. Mr. Lourenco had also acquired a tendency to purchase expensive art magazines at the bookstore, because he wanted to be the sort of person who bought glossy, high-art magazines and read them in a park, even when they hadn't made the rent for their apartment and the landlord had already knocked at their door a couple of times.

When Mr. Lourenco said that he'd identified a boarding

school in Bombay for pilots, Alex ignored him. There was no point in being a dog that chased after cars. Upward mobility, a term he often read in newspapers, wasn't for people like them. He told Mr. Lourenco that he wanted to stay at home and find a driving gig. Mr. Lourenco said they could talk more later, as though Alex would change his mind, after they snuck into the inauguration of the Goa airport.

On the day of inauguration, Mr. Lourenco put on a blazer he borrowed from his friend Natwarlal. It fit his arms but barely covered his sides. There'd be a ribbon-cutting ceremony followed by the takeoff of the first domestic flight from Goa to Bombay later in the day. Mr. Lourenco walked around the apartment thinking out loud about how he might best pull this off. The leather shoes he had weren't in the best shape, well-worn and rat nibbled. He didn't have good pants either, but he hoped the blazer would dazzle security into not looking anywhere below his distinguished belly. How does one know a babu? By his belly, of course. He laughed at his own quip.

Security barricaded the road leading to the terminal. A sizable crowd had already gathered. Politicians in cars were allowed to go through. Beyond the barricade, select people lined up on either side of the road clutching garlands. It was an important milestone for the state, and the ruling party wanted to be sure that it got credit. As expected, the police stopped Mr. Lourenco and Alex at the barricade. No entry for civilians, they said.

Mr. Lourenco remained resolute and told the guards he was a government executive making a film on the opening of the airport. What kind of film? they asked. An advertisement with a horse in front of the airport. A horse? they said, confusion writ large. To show the world how Goa evolved from horse carriages to airplanes, Mr. Lourenco said. Where's the horse? they asked. Just then, Mr. Lourenco's friend Natwarlal arrived with a brown horse in tow.

The police stepped away from the bristling horse and let them through. Past the blockade, Alex marveled at the ingenuity of this scheme. How would anyone remember to ask about filming equipment when a majestic brown horse was trotting in front of them? They had no reason to suspect Mr. Lourenco and Co. Why else would anyone bring a horse to the airport?

Natwarlal, who worked at the racecourse, filled Alex in on the details. This horse was worth several thousand rupees. He'd slipped him out for a couple of hours; he claimed to have done it for Mr. Lourenco, for whom he'd do anything, but Alex knew his talk to be just that for the most part, and they marched past the terminal to the adjoining farmland. Mr. Lourenco knew they'd never be allowed inside the terminal. His plan was to go around it and see the action from the front lines. They stood on the other side of the runway and watched.

A plane appeared in the sky. It slowly dipped, an eagle swooping from the sky. Alex looked at Mr. Lourenco. His eyes were on the plane, his hands leaning on the fence adjoining the runway, his right leg lifted up against the fence like a plane that might take off at any moment. He turned to Alex and said that their view was probably better than the one from inside the airport lounge. This is our lounge, he said.

The plane approached the runway, still dipping, and wind flew in their faces. Alex heard a distant neigh and looked back and saw the reins lying on the grass. The horse had bolted. Natwarlal shrieked, and all of them ran after the horse. Natwarlal ran behind Mr. Lourenco, cursing, You're finished! None of them saw the plane land.

When Alex finally caught up to the horse and offered it

several ripe bananas, Natwarlal held it, and Mr. Lourenco sighed in relief. I'd have been jailed today, Natwarlal said. That was the end of his friendship with Mr. Lourenco.

But Mr. Lourenco had no shortage of friends. A network of bus drivers and janitors and clerks all doted on him. When they had any problem—a runaway cousin or a missing bride or the usual depression—Mr. Lourenco would be there before they could think to call for him, and he'd take leave only after satisfactorily addressing the problem at hand. It was with the confidence of their support that Mr. Lourenco promised Alex that he'd arrange the flight school tuition, no problem. All I want, Mr. Lourenco said, is to sit on a plane and tell the person next to me that the pilot is my son. I promise, one day, we'll fly together.

When Mr. Lourenco paid Alex's tuition and wouldn't tell him how he'd arranged the money, Alex suspected a borrowing scheme involving a large number of people. But he didn't dwell. Flight school took up most of his time, and Alex had other things to worry about.

On Alex's first birthday away from home, Mr. Lourenco surprised him at the Bombay Flying Club by showing up at the dorm at midnight with a chocolate guava cake. The cake felt a little soggy and was heavy on the chunks of guava, but nobody at the dorm complained. Cake beat no cake. Technically visitors were not permitted inside the premises, but Mr. Lourenco had befriended the guards. After that, he visited every Sunday and lingered around the institute, chatting up Alex's classmates, trying his best to sneak into the simulator lab.

Which seemed to be affecting how the instructors treated him, Alex thought one day, peeing in a urinal at the institute.

They were always scolding him for the smallest of mistakes and using him as an example when they were teaching other students what not to do, even when he was free-styling on an X189 device. Somehow he'd been anointed the class clown.

Then he saw it. Someone had written his name on the wall above the urinal. ALEX LOURENCO. Next to random graffiti, tits, a penis between the tits, there was his name, scratched into the wall. Below it, the person had written TOUCH and some cuss words. Alex wondered who in his cohort had the time and interest necessary to prank him. He'd been a quiet presence for the most part, taking everything in. Was someone daring him to touch a dirty toilet wall? It didn't make any sense until he remembered how Dr. Iyengar, a faculty member, seemingly took care not to touch the hydraulic steering switch in the exact spot he had touched first.

For a long time, Alex had believed himself to be one-eighth Portuguese. It was an assessment based on Mr. Lourenco's version of their history, of his grandmother being one of the last órfãs do rei. And "Lourenco" pointed to Portuguese origins. He hadn't thought too much of the way some of his school classmates dissuaded him from coming to their houses, or the way people looked at his face when he said his name, or the way Mr. Lourenco stood at a respectable distance from the owner of the Tourist Bus Company. It wasn't as though he had no idea of their social status—he'd always known on some level but had never really thought about it. Mr. Lourenco had always told him that people didn't like anyone *different* from their own background, and he'd bought into that. Into them being outsiders and philosophers, not your regular Indians. But of course, he was no Portuguese Christian, he was no proper Catholic, he belonged to a Dalit family that took on a Portuguese surname—he was a fucking untouchable.

It was obvious. He didn't speak Portuguese; he had dark skin, a snub nose, a round face, and full lips. Everything about his Portuguese identity was a lie. He'd just been stupid enough to believe his father.

The following weekend, Alex got on a bus and went home. Mr. Lourenco had not come to the bus station to pick him up, so he walked to their apartment. He found it locked. He asked their neighbors for the key and stepped inside. The apartment had been turned over in search of something. Bedsheets crumpled in a corner. Documents spread on the mattress. The TV they had, an old model that needed to be slapped every two minutes for the picture tube to work, was missing. And then Mr. Lourenco came out from the bathroom, smiled, and remarked that Alex was home early.

Alex asked Mr. Lourenco why the apartment had been locked from the outside. Mr. Lourenco said that he'd asked the neighbors to unlock the apartment when it was time to pick Alex up at the bus station. He'd done that to be inaccessible to the man who lent him money. I told him next month, but he isn't listening, Mr. Lourenco said. Money you borrowed for my school? Alex asked, and Mr. Lourenco told him not to worry. That he'd take care of it.

It was at this point that Alex lost his cool and yelled at his father. What will you take care of? You can't even take care of yourself, he said.

Alex glanced at the documents on the mattress.

What are all these documents?

Mr. Lourenco said that the Portuguese government was offering citizenship to Goans of Portuguese descent. Wouldn't it be great to apply and move to Lisbon?

Alex understood immediately that Mr. Lourenco had falsified paperwork that proved their Portuguese ancestry.

Mr. Lourenco continued to explain: Banks in Lisbon, unlike banks in this great nation we live in, give out student loans even if you don't have assets.

Alex couldn't believe it. We're really Portuguese? he said, rising from the ground.

Mr. Lourenco took Alex's hand and began to say that his grandmother was white-looking, that she was fairer than most people. Alex wrangled free and said that being fair didn't mean anything. Mr. Lourenco gazed at the floor, and Alex understood that he'd arrived at a topic his father didn't want to discuss.

Why? Alex asked. Why lie to me? Why believe this shit when you know? What's wrong with being who we are?

Hypothetically, you know, Mr. Lourenco said, his eyes turning moist.

Alex threw the documents at Mr. Lourenco. You forged birth certificates?

Alex stepped out of the apartment. The dorm room in Bombay—his father paid for room and board—wasn't his. He had nothing, no completed degree, no job prospects. He didn't have anywhere to go, but he felt like going somewhere far.

He'd barely walked a couple of miles when he ran into a friend of Mr. Lourenco's. The guy, a janitor, congratulated Alex on becoming a pilot in training, and he credited Mr. Lourenco with the accomplishment because clearly the man loved his son more than God loved Jesus. Alex had merely smiled and bidden the man goodbye, but it depleted him, like he'd been robbed of his rightful anger, and the feeling would not leave him. It was as though he had a terrible sickness. He had an urge to vomit; he bent over by the roadside and opened his mouth to expel, but nothing came out. He roved the beach and kicked sand at the approaching waves, and as he did so, he felt the need to vomit return. A tearful Mr. Lourenco found him at the beach and grabbed his shoulder and said that all his life people had told stories about who he was. Chamar. Dalit. Untouchable. Bus driver. Converted Christian. Low-class buffoon. He wanted the dignity of telling his own story, the way he wanted it to be.

You're not making any sense, Alex shouted at him. He continued to yell while the wet fat mess that was his father kissed his forehead. Whoever he and his father were, they were bound together.

When Alex turned twenty-five, Mr. Lourenco made another promise. Alex had been refusing to say anything to Mr. Lourenco about whom he was dating. He had his reasons. Nothing had prepared him for the happiness Lara brought him. He wanted to marry her. He spent all his mornings typing into his phone. For the first time in his life, he had someone other than Mr. Lourenco, something Mr. Lourenco had no part in. But even that, Mr. Lourenco threatened.

First, he wanted to know whom Alex was always texting (a woman or a man?), what the nature of their relationship was (more than a crush?), how he'd met her (she dry-cleaned your jacket?). Next, he wanted to meet her. Alex wouldn't give in until Mr. Lourenco promised not to intervene *too much*. Then he wanted to see her again. And again.

He found out that Alex got off early on Tuesdays and would show up at his work just in time to join him and Lara at the movies. He taught himself about the business of dry-cleaning and accosted Lara with questions about it. He accompanied her whenever she went grocery shopping. And increasingly, the poor woman would look at Alex, a question in her eyes: *Is this a package deal?*

Alex told her on an afternoon they'd salvaged for themselves that it wasn't simple. He couldn't tell Mr. Lourenco to stop inserting himself into their lives. That's him, he said with a laugh, but Lara didn't seem amused. She told him what else Mr. Lourenco had been up to. He'd been visiting her at the store and trying to get on good terms with her boss. He'd been discussing things they hadn't had a chance to talk about. He wanted to know what kind of wedding she'd want, *hypothetically* want.

He agreed with Lara that chrysanthemum decorations were in vogue, although he knew nothing about them, and casually asked her what she thought about a flight-themed wedding. Left alone, he'd pick out names for our children, Lara said, holding her head.

Alex said he'd speak with Mr. Lourenco. What was he to do?

Time had given him some perspective, he said, pacing in front of Lara. Without his father, Alex said, he would've been on the streets. If Mr. Lourenco hadn't borrowed money and forged documents and secured loans for his studies, he'd never have been a pilot. He'd never starved for affection, for love. And it was his duty to give his father exactly what he needed, to ensure *he* had the best possible life.

So, he appropriated your life, and now the two of you will appropriate mine? Lara said.

Alex began to say that he wouldn't allow Mr. Lourenco to do anything that Lara wouldn't want, and Lara laughed at him. She said that she understood the delicacy of the situation, but Alex sensed a degree of resentment in her laugh, and he wanted to do something about it.

How do you feel about a week for ourselves, just the two of us? he asked. To take a stroll on Juhu beach, catch a late-night movie, and walk down Nariman Point holding hands, thinking about a wedding? He'd accrued some training rewards; he could use them toward a round trip on a commercial flight. Knowing Mr. Lourenco's long-standing desire, they could send him on a plane somewhere.

Lara smiled. She thought it best that they visit her parents at the same time and get their permission. They were conservative Christians, her parents. She said that Mr. Lourenco's exuberance would throw them off. Alex agreed.

Two weeks later, Alex waved goodbye to Mr. Lourenco at the terminal. He had never seen him so excited. Mr. Lourenco had held off on everything to pay for Alex's training, and he hadn't anticipated being able to fly so soon. He bobbed past security.

Alex turned back. He exited the terminal and took a phone call from Lara. She'd told her parents about their plans to visit. And they wouldn't hear of it. Her parents had received a proposal, she said. Someone they knew very well. They would drink a can of pesticide if she married someone who wasn't a *proper* Christian. She hated them for speaking that way, but she was afraid they'd follow through on their threat. She didn't want their death on her conscience.

Alex didn't know what to say; his head hurt. He tried to reason with her, but then an ambulance drove up, and she couldn't hear him in the commotion. He hung up. Someone had collapsed inside the airport and the paramedics were rushing them somewhere. The person lying on the stretcher had the same shirt as Mr. Lourenco. Alex ran. Paramedics slapped an air mask on the patient's face and loaded him into the van. It was Mr. Lourenco, motionless.

Alex jumped into the van and watched the paramedics connect wires to Mr. Lourenco's chest. Then they began to do chest compressions. As he watched, Alex imagined what he'd say to

Mr. Lourenco when he inevitably woke up—he wouldn't talk to him at first, what a scare he'd given him. Mr. Lourenco was going nowhere without boarding a flight, definitely.

But Mr. Lourenco flatlined. Alex stared at his going eyes.

Years later, on a commercial flight to Goa, Alex turned off the transponder and looked at the copilot. No westerlies, just as he'd predicted. They'd established contact with the airport and received a ten-minute hold. He glanced at passengers through the cockpit window, half expecting Mr. Lourenco to be there.

The plane hummed through small puffy clouds. Alex started the holding pattern and turned the plane around, speaking with the copilot about the rise of autoland in commercial aviation and how that would take away most of what they did. Landings were the only time they had any serious work. In a few years, they'd become standbys watching the plane land itself. It's a shame, the copilot agreed.

Alex's eyes fell on the passenger list. It contained the name and seat number of every passenger on that flight. From time to time, he looked at all the names he flew from city to city. To what faces they belonged, he didn't know. Sometimes, he'd remember a name or two from the lists he hauled off the plane. These names, they'd knock on his mind when he sat alone in his hotel room thumbing through TV channels. Or when he stood pressing his jacket; he'd given up on dry-cleaning forever. They'd pop into his head and check themselves out a little later. But they weren't permanent like "Paul" was. He'd never bothered with it when Mr. Lourenco was alive, but ever since the funeral his name had taken on a new meaning in his brain. An entire past buried in a name he'd never gotten to say.

He scanned the passenger list for "Paul" and almost always there was one, but never Mr. Paul Lourenco. There could never be. This Paul, he never left Alex's imaginings. Or said anything to him. But Alex sensed he was in there somewhere. He felt it every time he walked past Qureshi's Café and his eyes fell on the table where they used to sit. He felt it keenly the day he went to the apartment and packed up Mr. Lourenco's old clothes and documents and sat on their old mattress. On the wall, Mr. Lourenco smiled out from their photo at the zoo. A cold breeze stroked his arms, and Alex pulled one of Mr. Lourenco's shirts over him, and something inside told him to get up and run before he sank into the mattress forever.

The copilot kicked back his feet and signaled to Alex for the transponder; it had already been turned off. The guy leaned back and closed his eyes, and Alex called in to the cabin to begin his pièce de résistance. He sparked the intercom to play light music and spoke into the microphone. He announced himself, Captain Alex Lourenco. They were just over thirty kilometers from Goa International Airport. Current weather conditions were peachy, but the wait to land was ten minutes long. They'd sat waiting for a long time, he knew the last minutes of a flight were often the most frustrating, he assured them it'd be over soon. He hoped they'd had a great experience so far, the best possible one given the circumstances. In the meantime, he had some programming for them. The plane descended a couple thousand feet, and to the left far below, one could see the oval-shaped thing that was Magnificent Rock. Call it by any other name, it'd still be magnificent. Oohs floated through the cabin phone, and they brought Alex a little bit of Paul. Coming next, the Unflowering Gardens.

ACKNOWLEDGMENTS

Thank you to Jin Auh for believing in me from the beginning and guiding me here. And gratitude to Elizabeth Pratt and Abram Scharf at the Wylie Agency. Thank you to Naomi Gibbs, my dream editor, who saw this book exactly as I envisioned it and made it so much sharper. Her insights deepened this book. Also grateful to the brilliant team at Pantheon: Lisa Lucas, Natalia Berry, Michiko Clark, Sarah Pannenberg, Altie Karper, and Cat Courtade.

The MFA program at the University of Michigan gave me so much, and I'm particularly thankful for the mentorship of Peter Ho Davies and Akil Kumarasamy. Peter for the craft and wisdom. And Akil for everything—she is my hero. My supremely talented cohort: Annesha Mitha, Asher Dark, Carl Lavigne, Charlotte Rutty, Cherline Bazile, Karolina Letunova, Logan Lane, Meagean Dugger, Sarah Duffett, Sofia Groopman, and Zahir Janmohamed—I've so much love and admiration for them.

Thank you to the friends who impacted this book one way or another: Gerardo Sámano Córdova, 'Pemi Aguda, Dur e Aziz Amna, Laurie Thomas, Thea Chacamaty, Elinam Agbo, Mant Bares, Coleen Herbert, Joumana Altallal, and many others in the Michigan community. For conversations and vital feedback:

Yasmin Adele Majeed, Christine Vines, Gabriel Mundo, Melanie Pappadis Faranello, Katie Field, and Joanna Margaret. Special thanks to Farha for reading the early versions of these stories and supporting me. Thank you to the friends who've been rooting for me: Mridul, Kristen, Mourya, Manogna, Santosh, Vamsee, Sriram, Prudhvi, Harsha, Nayan, and Alyssa.

Thank you to PEN/Dau and the Key West Literary Seminar for making me feel like a writer. *VQR* and *The Georgia Review* for publishing my stories. Gerald Maa for the conversations, and the drink! I'm grateful to all my teachers: Garth Greenwell, Paul Yoon, Laura van den Berg, Elizabeth McCracken, Rebecca Schiff, Danielle Evans, Fernanda Eberstadt, and Michael Byers. Thank you to Julie Buntin and Van Jordan for the kindness and care. Shout-out to Suzanne Rivecca, who got me into fiction and changed the course of my life.

My father loved books before I did. My mother would have tried to read this book. My grandparents who raised me. This book is for them. All my family, blood and otherwise—thank you for traveling with me. Nanna, I hope this book is worthy of you.

Meghana, thank you for the life-sized blanket. You keep me from freezing in the cold.

Finally, Saavi: I couldn't have done it without you. Everything I write is for you.